JOHN F. DEANE was born on Achill I
founded Poetry Ireland and its journa
has published several collections of poe
Prize for Irish Poetry in 1998. *In the Nar*

OTHER BOOKS BY JOHN F. DEANE

FICTION

Free Range, short stories, 1994
One Man's Place, novel, 1994
Flightlines, novel, 1996

POETRY

The Stylized City, 1991
Walking on Water, 1994
Christ, with Urban Fox, 1997

TRANSLATIONS

The Wild Marketplace, from the Swedish of Tomas Tranströmer
For the Living and the Dead, from the Swedish of Tomas Tranströmer
The Distribution of Bodies, from the French of Jacques Rancourt
At the Devil's Banquets, from the French of Anise Koltz

In the Name of the Wolf

JOHN F. DEANE

THE
BLACKSTAFF
PRESS

BELFAST

First published in 1999 by
The Blackstaff Press Limited
Blackstaff House, Wildflower Way,
Apollo Road, Belfast BT12 6TA, Northern Ireland
with the assistance of
The Arts Council of Northern Ireland

ARTS
COUNCIL
of Northern Ireland

Reprinted 2000

Typeset by Techniset Typesetters, Newton-le-Willows, Merseyside

Printed in Ireland by ColourBooks Limited

A CIP catalogue record for this book
is available from the British Library.

ISBN 0-85640-640-6

www.blackstaffpress.com

1

She woke out of nightmare, her body wet with perspiration, her breathing difficult. There was a pale night-light in the centre of the ward that cast a yellow fog over the beds and their restless occupants. She hesitated, listening to know if the distant calling that had wakened her would repeat itself but the only sound outside the ward was of nurses talking together in the corridors, at their night stations.

Fear came over her again – she sat up in bed and tried to control it. She must not cry out, she would wake the others, there would be a fuss, the nurses would scold her, it would go down on her chart for the doctors to see. A black mark. They would tut-tut-tut at the end of her bed, consulting with one another, immaculate hands in the pockets of immaculate white coats.

She slipped out of bed and heard the slup slup slup of her feet on the linoleum as she went over to the big window. She saw herself approach, a wasted figure, small and frail, her once-rich hair now patchy and almost grey, the skull showing through. Beyond her pale image in the glass there was only darkness. Almost now, almost, she could see through her body into the darkness beyond. She put her hands up around her face and pressed herself to the window, trying to blot out the images from behind her. Out there, in that blackness, there was freedom, waiting . . .

And then she knew, with a sudden clarity that almost made her laugh aloud. She knew what she must do. It was so simple, why had she not known it long before, when she was stronger and more prepared? She turned – and met the terrifying eyes of an old woman fixed on her from the corner bed, eyes red and moist from their knowledge of pain, the twig-like fingers clutching a sheet to the withered chin, the sunken mouth fallen open in a half-grin of complicity. The small face seemed to come alight for a moment with malice and the mouth opened wide as if to call, but all semblance of awareness died in an instant and the old woman turned away into her cave of indifference.

She went back to the bed, put on her slippers and dressing gown. She looked out into the corridor. Here, too, pale night-lights made a looming tunnel of the world. The nurses' station was further down the corridor and the bright light within cast its net out over the floor and walls. A big round electric clock reached out, the second hand moving soundlessly. If they caught her out of bed they would handle her cruelly, their big bodies behind the hard white of the uniforms would overwhelm her and she would know again how brittle her bones had become, how easily her flesh could tear under the blades of their fingers.

She moved quickly out of the ward, turning away from the night station, reaching the marble floor of the landing. She was breathless already. And cold. A dark stairway led down from where she stood. She would not go that way. Too many doors. The open maw of the lift faced her. She stepped inside and it lit up for her. The doors sighed shut. She pressed the down arrow. There was a small mirror at face level and suddenly this tiny, enclosed world was the brightest she had been in for a long time. When had she worn lipstick last or known the joy of perfume on her body?

The lift stopped. The doors slid open. Softly. Ground floor. She had been up there too long, too far from the soil. The lighting now was soft and welcoming. She began to glide along the corridor, keeping close against the wall, towards the great front doors. Other doors, closed and threatening, suggested clinics, theatres, laboratories. The doors of the lift clicked shut behind her. Startling her. She felt very cold, the blood in her body inadequate to its task. There was a stronger light shining from the windowed night porter's office near the door. A small door was ajar in the wall beside her. She pushed it, cautiously. The faint light from the corridor showed her an aluminium bucket, mops, overalls, goloshes. Eagerly she put on a pair of dark blue overalls; they smelled of polish and detergent, of the normal, living world. The world of gossip and busyness and fuss. The goloshes, big and shiny black, she carried with her. She felt warm. Almost happy?

An elderly man was sitting behind the thick glass wall, his head heavy on his chest, his eyes closed. Behind him a telephonist's console. Any moment the lights might wink, a bell shrill. She tried the high, wooden front door. It was unlocked. Her God was with her. She was out on the steps. A faint light followed her from within, offering a small triangle of light she could set out on. There was a streetlight down along the avenue, among trees.

Soon she was running, still carrying the goloshes, on the smooth tarmacadamed avenue, her slippers loose about her feet, trying to trip her up. She hit her foot against a stone and cried out, quickly stifling the cry. She drew in among the shadows, a shadow among others, waiting. The great door had swung shut behind her. It was a closed mouth. Silent. Indifferent. Dark again. She put on the goloshes over her slippers and moved, more slowly, along the edge of the shrubbery. The trees were kind, whisperful and encouraging. And then she saw the gates, the high pillars with small lights on top of them, and beyond – release was waiting, freedom and hope. She turned back a moment and saw the hulk of the building, like a dragon, windows here and there barely visible, like scales on the dragon's flank. She laughed; she had not been changed to stone, or salt. She remembered the open mouth of the woman in bed and she shuddered; but she was leaving behind her that ward of blood, and those who had been born out of blood. She stepped, deliberately, out onto the road.

2

It was wartime still in the world. Late in 1941 a Focke-Wulf bomber, seriously damaged, was struggling back towards its base in Norway after escort duty in the Atlantic. It jettisoned its load of bombs which fell on the northern coast of the island, exploding on the slopes of the mountain. Tons of rock and clay were torn out by the explosions, leaving exposed the black inner layers that had been formed millennia before. The flank of the mountain burst into flames and the fire burned ferociously for hours, gratefully, as if something terrible had been waiting for such a fire, for such ashes, like the phoenix, to be reborn.

For days, so that it appeared the world would never again be able to gather itself back up. Landslides and slippages continued; rocks and stones and scree came coursing down into the waves, trickles of clay and shale followed, gusts of wind triggering further slides until great areas of fault were uncovered. Only after several weeks did the mountainside settle back into a semblance of quiet.

Here and there, on exposed slopes where only mountain goats and straying sheep found step, the leering face of metal, the jagged edges and scorched black shells of the bombs appeared. Things dripped and shifted along the shattered nerves of the mountain. By day disturbed sea birds – gull and chough and fulmar – screamed and swooped along the new cliff ledges, seeking grip. The winter winds clawed with long broken nails at the raw surfaces. The great wound in the mountain's flank lay open to the salt winds; cauterised; blackened; and the island shivered in its pain.

Those were years of war. Wolf packs continued to prowl the rich Atlantic waters, searching out and finding easy prey. Admiral Dönitz, commander of a powerful fleet of U-boats, was feared as the people of lesser times had feared the wolf of Gubbio. Unescorted and convoyed merchant shipping alike fell victim, helpless as lambs before the ravaging packs. Wolf packs, silent, slavering, heartless, rose from the depths of the ocean to devour, mercilessly, and the Atlantic became a thing of suspicion, dread and slaughter.

Wolves.

Sharks, rather. Sharks. Because the wolf is a creature of the earth, of mountainsides and forests, of scrublands and prairies, of times and silences beyond reach, and of the human heart.

On 23 February 1943, a gunboat of the *Kriegsmarine* fetched up in Purteen Harbour, shouldering aside a few rickety trawlers to moor off the deeper quay. Out at sea there were gales, along the western seaboard there were storms. The rocks and land edges were treacherous, reaching suddenly like long arms beyond where they were supposed to reach, popping up out of the waves and vanishing again with a throaty laugh. The Germans tied up, glad to find some moments' respite from the slaughter.

For over an hour some members of the crew watched the approaches to the tiny harbour. The others slept. A few thistles stood against the wind; a donkey shifted his rump with the shifting whims of the rains and swayed, dulled and dripping, shouldering the day. Small pennants of sheeps' wool caught on the barbed-wire fencing and waved under the breeze.

By late morning a sheepish sun glowed grey on the grey horizon. Three cautious armed sailors made their way up the dirt track leading towards the village. And there, at the head of the road, Captain Cyril Thornton O'Higgins stood to greet them. He was big, plump and upright, standing like a vision before them in a daffodil yellow windcheater. The stray hairs on his already balding head waved drunkenly. He saw migrants like the wandering albatross tossed off their course by the freak urgencies in the Atlantic. Hesitant, they levelled their rifles. He brushed their weapons aside with contempt.

The Captain was holding his naval cap – an anchor embroidered in golden thread on the peak – in his left hand. He had bought the cap in a drapers in Scotland. He wore a genuine Aran cardigan under his windcheater and his big green waders were folded down to just above his knees. He had been pottering around in the harbour among the quayside treasures, escaping from home and claiming his right to be styled harbour master. The rain had been further excuse. He had retired to the shelter of the Atlantic Bar from whose dusty windows he had seen the bristling ship come in to dock and, there being no immediate sign of life, had been about to demand the necessary formal courtesies.

He was no fool, Captain Cyril Thornton O'Higgins.

'Gutenacht! Gutenacht!' he boomed at them. He stretched out his right hand in greeting and grasped the hand of the first sailor. He shook it vigorously. Then he shook the hand of the second wondering German and repeated his phrase from the phrasebook. Finally he grasped the commander about the shoulders and proceeded to pick his way through the phrases he had learned.

'Itch!' he said, pointing to his chest. 'Itch, Captain Cyril Thornton O'Higgins. Captain! Cap-i-tan! Itch.' He put on his cap and pointed to the anchor. He smiled and nodded to the bewildered dignitary, then, pointing at the chest of the German, he said: 'Du? Admiral Doughnuts? Nitcht? Nitcht?'

The German grinned and shook his head. A relieving, buttercup yellow light had blossomed in his head.

'Nein! Nein! Nein!'

The Captain took him by the arm and urged him up the track

towards the Atlantic Bar, offering his phrases in a vaguely conspiratorial way. He told the commander, in fluid German, that the weather is better in Hanover, that the water in the bathroom of my mother is not warm, that the city of Berlin stands not on the Rhine and that the trees in Bavaria are very high. He stood back to judge the effect. The Germans seemed moved; they nodded and approved. And then they all stooped through the door into the cavernous darkness of the Atlantic Bar.

'Beer!' shouted the Captain.

The room was fragrant and dim from layers of spilled stout and whiskey. The Germans sat on a wooden form along one wall; the floor was cement and not too smooth; on the shelves behind the darkwood counter were bottles of whiskey and gin, bottles of beer, packages of tobacco, tea, matches, nails, and a great side of ham hung from a hook in one corner. The Captain brought them bottles of porter and they drank greedily, slugging noisily from the bottles.

The Captain addressed them then, in English, standing at the bar and leaning back against it, a bottle in his hand. 'Mizzenmast!' he boasted. 'Poop. Headsail. Frigate. Jib. Bilge. Brigantine. Dhow. Sloop. Weather eye. Yardarm. Yawl.' The words came slowly out of his mouth, one by one, insistent, like big gold doubloons.

The Germans acquiesced, impressed.

'More,' the commander offered, in English.

The Captain was enraptured. He began again. 'Poop, masthead, funnel, deck . . .'

'Nein! Nein! Beer, more beer!'

The Captain paused. He considered. 'Money? Have – you – money? Haben du – Cash! um zu haben?'

'Money?' one sailor asked the other.

'Geld, aggh! Geld! Ja, ja, money.' The commander reached into his pocket and drew out a wallet, filled with photographs and notes. 'Deutschmarks!' he announced proudly, offering one of the notes to the Captain.

The Captain took it and fingered it dubiously. 'Ya-ya, money indeed! Not much good around here, I'd say, what do you think, Tony?' and he handed the note to the barman.

'Load o' dried-out shite, that!' Tony pronounced, smiling towards his guests.

'Shite, ja, shite!' one of the happy Germans agreed.

'Still an' all, Tony,' resumed the Captain, 'maybe we better humour the buckos.' He spoke rapidly, turning and smiling occasionally towards the invaders. 'We don't want them coming in here and causing trouble, now, do we? Next thing we know the English will be after them and we'll have a war on our hands. Take the shite and be grateful for it. Give them a few more bottles. Quick, man! We'll be heroes! Patriots! Like Pearse and Plunkett and the lads. For a few bottles of stout!'

More bottles of porter were produced and the rifles were left down under the form. The Captain began to sing:

What are the wild waves say – ay – ing,
Sister, the whole da – hay long?

The Germans began with some martial songs, standing and offering the salute to the pink-and-white side of ham. But soon the porter began to soften the no-man's-land of their minds and they sat again, indulging in some sentimental Tannenbaum ditties. Tears came soon enough, and photographs were produced and mulled over. After an hour the commander decided they had better be getting back to the ship. He produced several more banknotes and waved them toward the Captain.

'More Guinness!' he shouted. 'More! Für our comrades!'

The Captain hesitated. More? Tony ducked under his counter.

The commander seemed to understand. 'You like cowboyz?'

'Cowboys?'

'Ja! Ja! The boy von cows. Ja. Cow – boy!'

'Yes, yes, I like cowboys.'

The commander grinned. Then he took out his pistol, causing the Captain's heart to flutter. It was a Luger, neat, deadly, and the German emptied onto his palm a perfectly shaped silver bullet.

'Ein bullet!' he announced. 'Silber. Von American cowboyz! Von Vild Vill Hick-cock!'

He offered the bullet to the Captain, who handed it over to Tony behind the counter.

Tony muttered, 'Cowshite!' and smiled his strained smile towards the German.

They took a crate of bottles from under the counter and handed them to the sailors. There was a German whooping of glee and the invading army made its way back through a brighter afternoon to the boat. Under the form in the Atlantic Bar they left their two Mauser K98 rifles, regulation weapons, never fired.

The Captain watched them go, a grin of satisfaction on his plump, reddening face. 'Well, Tony, might have cost us a few shillings but we have saved our country from a mighty invasion!'

'We!' Tony retorted. 'Us! It's *my* Guinness they've gone off with. The cow-holes! And this stuff is only shite. Pure, dried-out cowshite.' He held up the German notes against the light from the window. 'Cowshite! Droppings from a gang of cowboys.'

He pasted the notes up on the wall around the smokey mirror at the back of the bar. Source of conversations for decades yet to come; stuff of myth and legend. He dropped the silver bullet, with an expression of utter contempt, into a tobacco tin he kept for dud coins among the whiskey bottles.

Gingerly the Captain took up the two rifles. 'One for you, Tony, and one for me.'

When he wandered down to the harbour in the darkness of evening, the Captain was in jovial mood. The gunship lolled on a gently heaving sea. From its bowels came the sounds of revelry, more Tannenbaum songs in German, bottles clinking against each other, tinkling through the tranquil evening like bells from high pastures where bright flowers bloom in a green paradise. Peace reigned throughout that little world. There was a moon riding over the horizon like a friendly guardian galleon; the night would be dry and calm. The Captain hitched up his trousers and sighed with satisfaction. By dawn, he knew, Purteen Harbour would be empty once again.

Nora Corrigan often wondered how it had come about that she had married Cyril Thornton O'Higgins. He had been working in those early years – something not too taxing in the hat factory – setting off by bus early on Monday morning, arriving home late on Friday evening. Oh yes he had been handsome, still was, in a floundering fish sort of way. And she had been intrigued by all that swagger, all that bluster. She had wanted to probe beyond it, to touch the still heart of the man. And she had pitied him, too, for his name. 'Cyril.' Followed by a pause, and then 'Thornton!' Insisted on. Followed by a further pause. 'O'Higgins!' Then he would bow: 'Cyril Thornton O'Higgins, at your service.'

They met at a social in the schoolhouse. Nora had loved socials; the chat, the camaraderie among the girls, how they giggled and plotted, how they enjoyed watching and dodging the boys, how they pointed out the style in galluses, in ganseys, the length of trouser leg, the local unconscious boardwalk fashions of the young island fishermen. She loved to dance, too, although most of the local boys were rough, heavy-legged, head-hanging, bungling things. Ostriches. Bulls. Jellyfish. Not so Cyril, who moved with a grace that made of him a plumper Errol Flynn. Cyril never asked Nora to dance; she was too independent for him, perhaps, too much above him in social standing – a solicitor's daughter and a hat factory labourer. Not to be; not in the ordinary run of the ordinary and predictable wheels of life.

Now Nora was sitting and dreaming by the shores of the lake. She knew that Cyril was somewhere back the island, at the harbour, no doubt, idling, preening himself, discoursing. Nora had the sheets from the house and was soaking them in the great enamel basin. The lake water was brown but it cleaned the sheets and gave them a gentleness that hushed the skin like the touch of bog cotton against the tip of a finger. Soon she would refill the basin, add the soap and stomp around on the sheets. The cool caress of the water against her ankles, the tickle of the bubbles against her shin, the soughing and gurgling of the sheets, the rhythmic movement she created – as in a slow dance with the world about her for her partner – all that helped her to escape from the moment and from the weariness of her days. The afternoon was still; on the moors and lower slopes of the hills there was peace, a hovering of heather scents, the gently swaying tips of bog fern; the world, for once, a real and friendly presence.

Eventually, one night, on impulse, she had gone over to Cyril Thornton O'Higgins and asked *him* to dance. She had crossed the great abyss to the men's side of the hall. Under the startled eyes of the other young women. Such things were not done, were, simply, NOT done. He had stood there, gaping at her. Stunned. Until she took his hand and drew him gently out onto the floor of the world.

A tiny revolution had been accomplished. She danced well and suddenly his legs had become soft branches under him. He blundered, he stooped, he slithered; the floor of incipient love was almost too slippy for him. They sat down and began to talk. He rushed in at once, to tell Nora about his mother.

'She died, you know,' he said, 'when I was only five. It was TB she had. All the people were in the house for the wake and they ignored me. I went into the bathroom, poking around. I saw this bottle and I thought it had something like lemonade in it and I put it to my mouth and was going to drink it when this well-dressed young woman came rushing up the stairs and in through the open door of the bathroom and knocked the bottle out of my hands. Then she went away as suddenly as she had come, never saying a word. And I know, to this very day I have no doubt about it, that that woman was my mother. No other. And do you know what was in the bottle? Lysol. That's what it was. Lysol. Deadly!'

He had paused, watching her reaction. It seemed to be a test, an introduction, a query. She reached out and touched him gently on the shoulder. Then he smiled at her and invited her to the cinema in Westport; she had rarely been to the cinema; she accepted; she was caught!

During the bright days of their courtship, as they danced the ritual dances about each other, life was exotic and rare and all trace of her depression disappeared; she felt as if she had come out from behind the thick glass wall that had always separated her from peace and happiness, as if that cloying heaviness in her whole being had lifted through her, like some malevolent spirit that had been inhabiting her bones. She was beautiful then, vivacious, adolescent, whole. As if love could conquer all, even the invisible, intangible forces that keep the human soul in wearying subjection to their laws.

Once she had asked him back to her house. Cyril had been overawed at the comparative splendour of the Corrigan home and had sat foolishly silent while Nora's parents chatted and drank tea. At a loss, they asked Nora to play the piano for Cyril. She began, coyly, playing 'The Maiden's Prayer' and suddenly Cyril took two of the big silver soup spoons from the sideboard where they had stood sentinel, for years, among the never-used tureens and tankards; he stood beside her, a big smile on his face, keeping time with the spoons on the polished wood of the piano. Nora loved the sense of joy and ease the rattling of the spoons created in the fusty old house and only afterwards noticed the many little dunts he had inflicted on the piano. Mrs Corrigan was annoyed and showed Cyril the damage he had done. That had decided Nora; seeing how hurt he was, she promised herself there and then that she would marry him if he asked her to.

Nora watched the gently rippling surface of the lake. The water was dark in amongst the hillocks of peat, the bottom soft and black and treacherous. The old people said the lake was bottomless, that you would sink and sink for ever through the thick sucking mud. And out of that mud, the elders said, there rose the giant otter, the monster horrible beyond belief that would swallow any boy or girl foolish enough to venture out in tub or raft onto the waters of the lake. The children's lives were cluttered with fierce and unimaginable monsters.

She sighed and stepped into the big basin with the sheets. She would treadle here for a while, change the water again, and then treadle about once more. She would spread the sheets out on the rocks at the lake shore edge to dry in the wind and sun. How like the depths of that lake were the depths of her own heart. If only, if only the monster would rise out of those depths within her and be hunted down and destroyed. But things, she knew it only too well, were not as easy as that. It's a question of *nerves*, Cyril insisted, nerves, that's all, and a bit of happiness in your life will cure all that. She had allowed a light into her soul at his words. She had laid her life down beside his on that small hope, when hope was a tiny shoot, creamy-white before the hot breathing of the sun or the searching nails of the wind began to touch.

She spread the sheets out on the rocks; they billowed gently in the breeze. She put stones along the edges to keep them down. The water at the lake's edge rippled to a light gold. The afternoon stretched ahead, still and warm. She shivered.

Bill Cassidy, chemist, and his friend, Don Nealon, merchant, worked their way up along the southeastern flank of the mountain. It was early March 1945.

Cassidy, a tall, gaunt man, his face the colour of wet salt, was beginning to age; in his shop he stood lugubrious behind his counter, no keen salesman. But he was generous, dispensing glucose sticks freely to any child who ventured into his shop, ignoring bills he felt his customers might find it difficult to meet. Cassidy's hands were griffon's hands, but brought electric joy to the necks of kittens he loved to keep and pet. Thick grey eyebrows shadowed keen but kindly eyes.

Nealon, brash, self-made man, was a plump and satisfied three-score, his white hair distinguishing him in business gatherings and functions around the west. His pleasure was to rest his hands atop his drumlin stomach and lean back in his chair after a hearty meal, puffing on his success and blowing rings of bonhomie into the air. Big red fists, the fingers strong and definite in emphasis, keen for the rolling of a cigar and for the gentle caress of a trigger.

Both men were dressed in warm hunting clothes against the shrill, demanding winds. They carried rifles, cartridge belts crisscrossed their chests and buckled about their waists. Hunters. For the thrill of it.

They climbed quietly, downwind of their hoped-for prey. Their waders sank in the winter-wet, wind-scorched grasses of the mountain. A bitterly cold wind came round the high reaches of the mountain, slicing down against them. The sky was grey and heavy as metal. Their faces were alert to the hunt and their eyes bright in anticipation of a kill. They reached the lower ridge on the eastern side and the great sweep of the Atlantic lay before them. To their left rose the high cliffs, the scarred face of the mountain.

The chemist, his body drawn up again in wonder before the awesome magnificence before him, stiffened suddenly. 'What was that, Don?' he whispered.

'What was what, Bill?' the merchant answered. 'I didn't hear anything.'

'Like a howl, or a bark or something, distant, up there on the face of the cliff. Somewhere.'

They paused, listening. There was nothing. Bill shrugged.

Slowly they worked their way up the slope of the cliff edge. To their right the fall was precipitous, down rocks and crags to the sea.

They were flies, tiny creatures stirring on the face of a vast creation. They crouched, lest too obvious a movement scare their prey into unreachable fastnesses. To their left the gentler slopes of the mountainside, heathers, lings and ferns shivering under the everlasting winds. They could see sheep huddled into shelters shrugged out under overhanging clay banks. Above rose the mystic height and power of the cliffs, two thousand feet above the level of the sea.

Once Bill stumbled and for a brief moment his life hung perilously free. A small shower of stones clattered from under his foot down over the cliff into emptiness. His left hand grasped at the unwilling grasses. A great panic shook him through. He steadied himself, breathing deeply.

'For frig sake, Bill!' Don hissed at him.

Bill looked up, surprised. The older man's face was flushed with anger.

'Go on! Give a fuckin' yell! Beat a drum! Do you want to tell the whole world we're here or what?'

Bill offered no response. He had never seen his friend like this. For a moment the two men glared at one another. Enemies. Then Don turned and they continued the climb.

They reached a high point from where they could see most of the daunting cliff wall. It rose beyond and above them like the end of the world; great wet gables of black rock, here and there the scrawny mosses and grasses that had found thin ledges of boulder clay to grow in. They paused, breathing heavily. For some time they scanned the area ahead of them, in silence. Nothing stirred. And then Don gripped Bill's arm, a harsh, biting grip. At the same time Bill heard it, too, a long, low wailing sound coming from somewhere on the cliff wall. The sound faded slowly, a long dying echo.

'Sounds almost human,' Don whispered.

All at once the stretches of the mountain, the might of the cliffs and the ocean, appeared immeasurably lonely, empty and threatening. Don's grip seemed now to be a reaching for comfort. Bill felt a terror catch him, his flesh suffered a biting rush of cold and he shivered violently. Then they heard it again, that echoing wail that seemed at once human and inhuman, utterly remote, yet close. Bill shook himself loose from Don's grip and began to move back the way they had come.

'Wait, Bill, wait. Don't be such a friggin' fool!' Don's voice was filled with venom.

Bill turned, sheepishly, but he was angry. 'Look here, Don,' he reasoned. 'No need to take it out on me. Don't call me a fool. I'll admit I'm shaken by that sound. That's all. No call for such language from the likes of you!'

'Well, let's see what it might be before we turn and run like buggerin' cowards.' Don was trying to be calm and rational, but he lifted his rifle and slipped the safety catch. He faced the cliff wall. 'It's no sheep, nor goat, that's for sure.'

'It could be an eagle, or an animal in pain, or . . .'

There was something rushing towards them from a ledge beyond; it seemed to appear from the very face of the cliff, as if it were born out of the dark power of the rock. Urgent and careless of its direction it bounded towards them. They saw at once it was a mountain goat, big and scraggy in its grey coat. It had a short beard and its large horns, raised like twin serrated sabres, curved beautifully. Sure-footed, but scattering scree down the cliff face as it came, it made swiftly and directly towards where the men were standing. After the initial shock of its appearance, Don raised his rifle and aimed. The creature did not flinch in its headlong dash. Don hesitated, unsure how to react to this approach across precipitous ledges towards them.

'Shoot! Shoot!' Bill urged.

It was too late. Both men had to leap quickly onto the grassy patch to their left as the animal rushed past, its eyes wide in terror, its leathery hooves dislodging stones and shingles. It vanished behind rocks below them. They heard its progress for some moments, the stones and pebbles falling, the fading clattering of its hooves.

Don gathered himself off the grass. He had dropped his rifle and fallen forward on his face. He was wet and frightened. He turned. Bill was standing above him, his rifle raised and aimed at Don's chest. There was hatred sculpted across his face.

'You awful fucking fool!' Bill shouted. 'You nearly had us both killed. Why didn't you shoot?'

Don bunched his fists. His impulse was to rush at the other man and bring him down before he pulled the trigger. For a moment they faced one another. And then they heard the sound again, a long mournful wailing that rose slowly in pitch and then stopped short, suddenly. As if cut clean through by a knife. It seemed to be nearer them, louder, from a ledge somewhere above.

'My Christ!' Bill said. 'What's happening to me? I'm sorry, Don, I'm sorry, I didn't mean to aim at you.'

Don's anger, too, had vanished.

'Let's get the hell out of here,' he said.

For a few seconds they stood, rigid with fear. There was silence, only the harsh breathing of the wind, the far-off throaty moaning of the sea. They began to ease back, slowly, downwards, the way they had come. They could see nothing on the cliff wall, no movement, no stir. Then they turned and began to run, slipping and sliding, their fear pounding along beside them.

When the immense shudderings of the war finally came to a halt and the world hung in an uneasy peace, Cyril Thornton O'Higgins escaped once more from the confines of his island and got a job with Maclean and Sons, Boat Builders, in Mallaig, in the northwestern Highlands of Scotland. He found lodgings in a small house in the town, on Cullinair Hill, a long street leading at an acute angle up into the sky from the water's edge. His landlady, Mrs Dunbar, was impressed with having a captain reside a while in her house but she did not have time to grow fond of her garrulous guest. He was fired after four weeks when it became clear that he knew nothing whatsoever about boat building. By then, in any case, he had grown weary of the daily climb back up Cullinair Hill every lunch time and again before supper and once more after his nightly visit to the All and Sundry.

He had just been called into the office at the dark end of the yard and told he was fired when a boy arrived with a telegram for him. The telegram saved the Captain's dignity. To have escaped from Nora's company even for half a season was an important achievement in his life and the race to Scotland, when the hay was saved and in the loft, when the turf was safely stacked away in the shed, had seemed the opportunity of a lifetime.

The Captain spent his final evening, skipping supper, in the All and Sundry. Here he dispensed his news and his largesse. The single malts were on him. The telegram was the arrival of the Holy Ghost to comfort him: he had a son, Paddy, and he would have to leave them to fulfil his paternal duties; sad and all as he was to go he had to be with his wife and son. They drank Bull's Blood and Sheep Dip and Holy Dew out of the Captain's pocket while he boasted of his adventures on the rough seas off the western coast and told how, single-handed, he had foiled a German invasion of England through the lower fields. He was hero for the evening and the malts were now returned to the Captain in grateful recognition for his services to the free world. He wept with pride and gratitude and felt how terrible a thing it was that he had to leave such wonderful hosts and companions. Still, didn't he have a son!

And he would bring him up as fearless, he promised the men of Mallaig, as courageous and generous as he was himself, he would become a leader of his country, a salmon among sand eels, a man among chickens, an oak among thorn bushes. As he wandered alone back towards his digs and turned with extreme reluctance to face up Cullinair Hill for the last time, the Captain praised God's expertise with the stars; he leant backwards to see the panoply better and found himself sitting heavily on the wet ground. He pissed against a tree and prophesied a great future for all upright men. He walked full face into a pillar box and apologised with wholehearted feeling to the grinning, forgiving mouth.

If only my own Nora could smile like that, dear friend, what a great boon that would be. But she won't smile like that, not she, no sir, not she, she has the bug, you know, that bloody wretched scut of a bug that they can't reach out of her, and she will cry and swoon, and grip my trouser legs and wish she were dead, or worse, dear friend, or worse. But now I have a son, out of these very loins, a son, I tell you, Paddy is his name, see, it says so here on the telegram, see, *Pat*, there written large and clear and he must do her good for she's been well and blossoming since I planted the seed in her womb. Yes, me, your one and only Captain Cyril Thornton O'Higgins, dear friend, dear, dear friend.

The Captain reached his arms around the pillar box and breathed his hot booze breath into its face, and sank slowly to the ground before it to sleep a perfect, holy sleep.

Patrick Lawrence Dineen – affectionately known as 'Puddings', 'Pat Larry', 'the Reek' – owned a small grocery shop on a headland on the wrong end of the island. It was an area populated by rabbits, furze and fuchsia bushes and a fistful of cottages. Not a great deal of business worked its way to that corner of the world, so Pat Larry Puddings the Reek brought his business out of the corner and into the world.

Pat Larry was big of body. Round-faced, his forearms strong as boulders, his small blue eyes looked out at the world with a mixture of apology and longing. To reach out to that world he had bought a high van and had fitted it out with shelving and cupboards; into these he loaded his groceries, his tea chest, his sacks of flour, sugar, meal, his weighing scales, his cans and bags and jars. He was proud of his van – it epitomised his progression into the new age from the ass and cart on which he had begun his forays out into the island. Up on the high forehead of the van he had painted the words: HERE COMES DINEEN – HE DELIVERS.

On Tuesdays and Fridays Pat Larry left his shop in the sweet and short-sighted care of his niece, Nellie the Gate O'Hara, spinster, tall and crooked, grown placid at last beyond the high fence of hope, and he drove a careful route that brought him up and down the lanes and highways to the front gates and the back gates of the island people, blowing his horn and selling, delivering and even bartering his precious goods.

One Monday evening Pat Larry loaded the van as usual to have everything in readiness for an early start. Tea chest replenished. A sack of white flour. His brown paper bags. His scoop. A large sack of sugar. The evening was still and warm. After heaving and ferrying he was huffing a good deal and he sat on the low stone wall on the other side of the laneway from his house. He could hear the soft murmuring of the sea beyond the headland; there was a skylark filling the glass bowl of the sky with its water music. The old fuchsia trees, bullied into scrawny, leaning shapes by the prevailing winds, breathed easily. He thought about the men's mission beginning Saturday evening; a Jesuit down from Gardiner Street was to give it. A Jesuit out of Dublin! That was something. He'd surely have news for them, here on the last outpost before the sky. News about the heart of man, news about the kind and forgiving heart of God. Pat Larry promised himself he'd make it to the chapel every evening and go to Confession on both Saturdays. Poor Father Crowe; he'd be fumbling in close pursuit of the Jesuit's back, like a black-backed gull following a trawler into port. Pat Larry would relish a good shake up for his fat soul, out of which shame and sadness grew, like weeds, ineradicable, persistent, with a million flowers of dust.

He sighed; he had problems, here on the edge of the world, far from the currents that swept life bubblingly along in the capital. He would like to brighten up his shop and home, some curtains, new gutters. But no woman would ever go for him in spite of his caring nature and his modest wealth; wasn't he Puddings, wasn't he the Reek, a pork pig, a tar barrel, a whale! This time, though, he'd tell the Jesuit about his sorry sinning in the lonely dark of his home, sin after sin after sin, followed by remorse and disgust and shame, and then again next evening – and the next – and the next. He could tell the Jesuit, he could ask for help, he would be unknown to a Jesuit out of Dublin, the priest would soon be back in the city and Pat Larry would never see him again.

Today Maud Tuohy, young and pretty and spry wee Maud, her twinkling eye and open, honest face coming like sunshine through the rain, had cycled past his shop in the early afternoon, and he had seen the soft white flesh of her thigh where her skirt had caught awkwardly under her on the saddle. The memory of it would cause him difficulties as he sat alone in the darkness beside the wireless, waiting for his time to sleep. That glimpse of flesh. Tonight again, he knew it, he would suffer that same disgust and despair within him that he would never, ever know the taste of a woman's flesh this side of heaven, or of hell.

Suddenly agitated, Pat Larry heaved himself off the wall and slammed shut the big back doors of the van. The sound echoed angrily through the peace of the evening. Then he walked as fast as his round frame allowed him down to the shore where the current went streaming past with a low, threatening animal growl. He watched a while over the water towards the darkening horizon. Sometimes here, in the calm evenings, a seal would lift its head out of its salt-water world and look towards Pat, and Pat would stare back, wondering, both creatures ignorant of one another, two worlds touching a moment and as quickly shivering apart. This evening there was no contact with that other world and as he came back up the lane and the midges nipped at his flesh, he could already see before him the glow of Maud's thigh shining like a lantern in the darkness of his brain; he knew that once again he was beaten, that before he could find sleep he would... His huge bulk sagged under the weight of sadness. He closed the door of his shop against the world outside.

In the morning Pat Larry made himself his usual Tuesday breakfast: three rashers, three sausages, a few slices of bread fried in the fat, and some plump slices of May M'Namara's luscious home-made black puddings. And tea. Cup after cup of hot tea scaffolded on several spoons of sugar. Nellie would be by at half past nine. By ten o'clock Pat Larry would be on the move. Delivering.

He stepped out into a crisp, clear sunshine, planting himself once more in action, in the world, bathing himself in the normality of light after the gritty embrace of darkness. Sometimes Pat believed there was the unsubstance of night in his veins, but in sunlight he blossomed like a huge jungle lotus.

He hesitated. The air did not seem right. There was a silver tension in the light, a heaviness in the still air that did not allow for peace. He felt the back of his head chill suddenly as if he were being watched from the very darkness he had left. He turned quickly. There was only the open door into his shop and through the shop the door into his kitchen. And silence. And emptiness. The stalwart smell of frying lingering on the air. Across the road the gnarled branches of the fuchsia trees were too bare to conceal anything of matter. Yet his sense of unease persisted. There was no sign of a living soul along the lane. He walked slowly to the side of the house.

The big back doors of his van stood ajar. The crusts and crumbs of his stores lay scattered over the sandy ground. The back wheel on the right-hand side was ripped and flat. The van stood at an unnatural tilt to the day. It was a scene of minor, irksome destruction. Pat stood transfixed before it, smitten by a horror that swelled rapidly within him. And then, gradually, he grew aware of a foul smell, a smell of putrefaction, of faeces, urine, blood; it seemed to emanate from the van and from the scattered items of the store.

He clenched his fists tightly by his sides, drew his large body together and let out a long frustrated roar. His head shook like a wild beast's with anger and disbelief. The world had shuddered before him, revealing within itself an essential fault. The possibilities of grace had been withdrawn. He imagined he heard an answering roar from beyond the walls and ditches of the foreshore behind the house. An early-morning echo, he thought, and dismissed it.

Holding one hand over his nose and mouth he went up to the van and looked inside. Everything had been torn from the shelves and presses and flung on the floor of the van or out onto the ground. Tins of fruit had been burst open and their contents had disappeared. Sugar, flour, tea, lay like thick dusts everywhere. The tea chest was smashed into pieces. He was horrified at the violence evident everywhere. Inside the van the stench was almost unbearable. Pat Larry staggered back out into the tainted morning and stood a while, his hands to his face, his life's veins hardening again with darkness. Nellie, simple, plain Nellie, stood at the corner of the house, aghast. Nothing like this had ever hit the island.

'It's the end of the world, Pat Larry,' she offered in a frightened whisper.

When Garda Vinnie Scollon arrived, a man caught in the ponderous slowness between youth and middle age, he propped his big Raleigh bicycle against the wall of the shop; without saying a word, but eyeing the destruction around the van, he stooped to take the clips from his trouser legs. He hung the clips on the bar of the bike, took off his guard's cap and draped it over the saddle. Pat Larry was sitting on the stone wall on the other side of the road. Nellie was standing in the black doorway of the shop. Drooped. As usual.

'Pat!' Vinnie's greeting was cautious, matt and business-like. The garda moved towards the van, drawing a notebook and fountain pen from his breast pocket.

Pat Larry got wearily off the wall.

Vinnie was wrinkling up his face. 'Strong smell,' he commented.

'A fuckin' stink! Note it, Vinnie!' Pat answered. 'The bastards were either filthy or sick or covered in shit, or both!'

Vinnie nodded gravely towards Nellie, who ducked back at once into the shop. He put down a few notes, glancing among the burst cans and packages scattered over the ground.

'Seem to have burst open the tin cans,' he commented. 'How do you figure they done that?' He picked up one of the cans, a tin of fruit cocktail. It was crushed in the middle and a hole had been ripped in its side. 'Make you think of an animal,' he muttered.

Pat Larry hesitated. 'Animal couldn't open the back doors of the van, Vinnie.'

Vinnie glanced at the door and then into the van. He gazed at the dim interior for some time. Gathering himself. 'Smashed it open. Smashed it. Wanton destruction, that's what it is. Wanton. Any money in the van, Pat?'

Pat climbed inside and went at once to a small wooden tobacco box on the floor of the van. It was broken but it still contained a few copper coins, some florins and one orange-yellow ten-shilling note. He held the box towards the garda.

'Not robbery, then,' Vinnie said, writing in his book. He glanced up at Pat. 'Animals,' he pronounced. He began to examine the ground about the van. It was sandy and soft. At one point he went down on his hands and knees. 'Let's see the soles of your boots, Pat.'

Pat Larry turned and lifted the sole of one big boot towards the guard.

'Them's the ones you wore yesterday?'

'Them's the ones. Th'only ones, Vinnie.'

'Notable pattern on them, Pat. Same as here.' He paused again. He rubbed his nose hard. He knelt on the ground, as if in prayer before the mystery of it. Then he came to his conclusions. 'That's it. Now. There's for you. They do be in it, Pat, they do be in it.'

For a moment he eyed the large shopkeeper with some suspicion. Pat Larry clenched his fists as he read the intimation in the other man's eye. Only then did the guard notice the tyre. He clambered awkwardly off his knees. He examined the tyre carefully. It was torn into shreds. One big gap showed where tyre and tube had been torn off.

Vinnie stood up again. 'Not human, that,' he pronounced. 'Not natural. Torn to pieces, the tough rubber. Not cut. Torn. Like great pincers. Like jaws.' He laughed then, nervously, at his own words. Pat Larry shook his head.

'And that stink,' Vinnie continued, 'not human, neither, not drink, nor sick, nor even dirt. Animal stench that, animal stench. A man and ay animal. Together. Done that, I'd say.'

He told Pat to make an inventory of what was damaged, to change the back wheel and bring the torn tyre and tube down to the barracks. Then he wrapped up two tins and a piece of the smashed tea chest in a piece of sacking and fixed them to the carrier of his bicycle.

As he stooped to put on his clips he said: 'You better clean up, Pat. And I'd wash out that van if I was you and disinfect every little bit of it, insides and outs. Jeyes Fluid, buckets of it. That's your man. Ay animal. Mad dog or something. Rabies. Who knows? Morning, Nellie' – he shouted the greeting into the darkness of the shop – 'morning, Pat. Be in touch!'

He pushed his bike, unhurriedly, onto the lane and mounted it. Pat Larry stood a while, watching him go down the lane, the soft ticking sound of the bike fading gradually into the late morning air. Cautiously, like a rabbit peering from the neck of its burrow, Nellie came back into the doorway, her hands rubbing idly against the cloth of her dark blue apron.

In her post office Dotie O'Grady was the first to know that Nora O'Higgins was close to delivering a child. Nora's voice, over the phone, was breathless, but calm. Quickly Dotie whirled the handle of her phone and called up Mrs Tuohy.

'Oh Mrs Tuohy, do you know what but Nora O'Higgins is just about to drop and himself of course is away in Scotland and I've no way of getting a hold of Pat Larry except Maud.'

'Now Mrs O'Grady,' came the reasoning voice on the other end of the line. 'What I gather from that is this: you need my Maud to go to Scotland to fetch the Captain?'

'No no no, Mrs Tuohy, what must be done is Maud is to go and fetch Pat Larry in the van to fetch Nora O'Higgins to the hospital at once if not before. And quickly if there's not to be an emergence.'

'Emergence, Mrs O'Grady? Or emergency?'

'The both, Mrs Tuohy, for God's sake, the both!'

Pat Larry was there when Maud called into his shop to explain what was requested. Before Maud the round man stood dumb, his hands becoming two great inert sides of ham, his heart working so that the blood rushed into his cheeks and neck. When he understood what was being asked he moved at once, eager and willing. He backed out his newly refurbished van onto the lane. He stopped at the O'Higgins home by the crossroads and helped Nora into the high seat beside him; he drove as if a saucer of water stood balanced on his roof, his right elbow bulging out through the opened window. The van smelled of disinfectant and tea leaves.

Less than half an hour from the hospital Nora asked him to stop the van. That particular stretch of road was potholed and the van, in spite of all his caution, rattled and shook; the child was insisting, she told him, that it would wait no longer. She asked Pat, please, to go for a stroll over the bog for half an hour or so while she lay down on the floor of the van, among sacks of sugar and boxes of spirits, the weighing scales, the groceries in their packages and tins.

And so, while Dineen's delivery van stood in at the side of the road on a patch of ground blackened with turf mould, Pat Larry walked slowly away, over the ditch, onto a soft cushion of heather and peat that began the long slope towards the Nephin mountains. The sun was low in the sky; the world was bathed in a gentle golden glow. The left side of the van, Pat noticed, was somewhat lower than the right, the road sloping towards the drain. In the distance the great pyramid of Croagh Patrick with the tiny bump of the chapel visible on top rose like a great blessing.

'It'll be a boy.' Pat Larry was certain, reading all the signs. 'And she'll call him after me and after the mountain, too!'

Heath and moor and evening silence. Not a breath of wind, not a sound from bird, beast or man. The fretful heart of the universe momentarily stilled in contemplation of the wonder of itself. Pat Larry found a low furze bush and sat down behind it on a mossy clump of earth. He could not be seen from the road but he could view the van through the thorns. Not a stir. Not a sound. He had expected screams, a violent rocking of the van; after all, something miraculous was taking place, something utterly momentous, a new life arriving on the earth. There was nothing. He took out his fob watch. Twenty minutes gone. He was getting a little cold. No house anywhere within view, no traffic on the road, not even the spittling sound of a bicycle across the distances. Pat Larry leant forward meditatively, his arms resting on his knees. This could be the very beginning of the world, he mused, emptiness, silence, distance, and – his van. His delivery van. The whole of creation seemed benevolent this evening, as if the great sore of original sin had never broken out on the soft flesh of humankind.

The van door opened, and there was Nora, waving. She carried a bundle in her arms, a new life wrapped in one of Pat Larry's flour sacks. Not a cry from the child; time stopped and the world enlarged. Pat was overcome. Without a word he took Nora's hand and kissed it, gently. Nora was pale and sweating. He helped her back into the van and settled her as best he could. He started the van, anxious even at the raucous sound of the engine as if some great injustice were being done to the moment. He pulled out onto the potholed road. He drove mother and child to the hospital in total silence, Nora leaning back against the tea chest, unspeaking, rocking quietly, the child quiet in her arms.

After he had handed them both into the charge of a nurse in the hospital, Pat Larry rushed to send a telegram to Captain Cyril Thornton O'Higgins: 'A BIRTH. PERFECT DELIVERY. PAT.' He looked at the words; that was not enough; he added: 'CONGRATU-LATIONS. DINEEN.'

There had only been one small anxiety in the birthing. The child emerged gracefully into the world between the raised knees of her mother and came to rest, after the long voyage, on a millet sack laid down on the floor for its welcoming. But the van being at such an angle to the world, the child had rolled, slowly, silently, bringing her birth cord with her, and had stopped against the groceries piled on the left-hand side of the van; the soft head had touched, ever so softly, the side of a large can of golden syrup, and the body was pulled softly by the pull of the cord still attached to the mother's life. Hardly worth mentioning, merely a slight indignity of which the child was totally unaware. But the Captain took up the detail in later years and used it as one explanation of the whole thing.

Pat Larry came out of the post office and looked up with immense satisfaction at the sign on the high forehead of his van: HERE COMES DINEEN — HE DELIVERS.

When the Captain got off the bus at the crossroads outside his house he had in his suitcase a pair of the smallest, most adroit football boots imaginable; he had a drum with a pair of drumsticks, on the side of the drum exotically painted Indians performed a war dance; he had a leather belt onto which was stitched a small leather holster with a fashionable clip and a silver-handled six-gun with several packets of caps that made real bangs. For Nora he had a Highland scarf, one, he was assured, that had belonged to Sarah Jane Emer Mac Taggart herself, of the original Mac Taggart clan of the Outer Isles.

He was handed down the suitcase from the roof of the bus.

'I have a son, you know, Willie, a son, and his name is Patrick,' he confided to the young bus conductor, Willie Quinn, as the latter climbed down from the roof of the bus. 'Pat, if you like. But we'll see. He might be bigger than a mere Pat, if you take a look at me! And then he might have the spirit of fun and frolics, like myself, and then he might be called Paddy. But then again, you see, he might be the studious and intellectual type, again like yours truly, and then he will insist on being called Patrick. All's to see, Willie, all's to see.'

The Captain had his chest out, his mouth open. Any minute now, Willie thought, he'll give a crow like a thriving cock. But the Captain turned to face the gate of home, straightened himself gamely, and went in to be welcomed by, and to welcome onto the earth, his own strong son.

Nora was going through one of her better times. She was happy to be working around the house with only her little child to keep her company. She had an old osier carrycot and she brought the child everywhere with her, transferring her to the big-wheeled pram when she went down the long sandy road to the stores. There Pat Larry beamed with a special delight as his great shadow stooped with the utmost caution over the pram and his enormous hand, one red finger outstretched, touched the child gently under the chin.

'That's my girl,' he chuckled. 'That's my girl.'

Nora had decided to call the little girl Patricia, and she whispered and hummed to her throughout the day. With the Captain away the small house at the crossroads had been a palace, the quiet scarcely disturbed, the chores light; Nora's body floated on the gardens, over the yard, onto the road. Patricia was a peaceful child and already slept a great part of the night; all was well. All manner of things had never been so well.

The Captain's sudden irruption through the back door struck Nora as a blow on the back of the neck. He was not due back until the spring when he should have gotten enough money together to see them through the year. Here he was, big and loud, filling all the house with his bluster. The Captain never opened a door, Nora used to say, he came through it, and at once the fire in the old Aga cooled a little, the lamp before the Sacred Heart flickered and went dim, the kitchen darkened as the curtains seemed to draw closer together, and the cat, Truelove, attempting a leap from the stool, cracked its chin and back-flipped under the table with an atrocious screeching while the front door banged shut before it could recover and get out.

'I'm back!' the Captain roared.

The pain at the back of Nora's head began at that moment as a dull ache, rather like the low-pitched beginning to a drawn-out, ever-rising scream. She froze in position, feeling a surge of resentment against the intrusion. She was leaning over the sink, washing nappies. She shook the water from her hands and reached for the towel before turning round. Composing herself. Reaching for strength out of the air. Patricia had begun to cry vigorously in her wicker basket, and Nora made for her at once.

'I'm back,' the Captain repeated, more quietly.

'Shush, love, shush, there now, there, there, there.'

Nora lifted the baby from her basket and held her tightly against her breast. Too tightly, perhaps, holding her for a few moments, just a few more moments to herself, before the demands of the Captain insisted on being met. The child screamed louder and Nora rocked her more wildly; the Captain put down his bags and suitcase and closed the back door after him, gently. Then he sat down on the ledge under the side window and waited. He was forgotten as Nora and child rocked together in an easing storm.

'There's a babba, there's a babba, there's a babba.'

Gradually the crying eased, the shushing became a pigeon croon, the kitchen settled back to peace. At last Nora remembered the Captain and smiled. She carried the baby over and sat down beside him on the ledge. Quietened, they kissed each other softly on the lips and she whispered: 'You're home early, you're welcome.'

She lifted the edge of the bonnet from the baby's face and opened the top of the blanket. The baby was almost asleep again, the worried, nervous crying still a quivering under the chubby cheeks and held in check, for the moment, under the shut eyes.

'My God, he's lovely!' the Captain whispered.

Nora handed him the bundle with reluctance and he held it out from him like a tray of cut-glass goblets.

'No, no, you hold him,' he said. 'I'm afraid I might break him, or let him fall.'

Nora took back the bundle. 'It's a girl,' she whispered. 'Our own little, sweet little girl.'

The Captain was stricken. But perhaps she was playing the pretend game. He looked at the child again, definitely a boy, a bit small perhaps, but a boy. 'Nora, Nora, Nora, it's a boy, and Patrick is his name. Paddy. Pat Larry sent me the name on the telegram.'

Nora put the child down into its basket without a word and lifted the long white robe to reveal the linen nappy, the huge pink pin. She opened the pin and drew back, gently, the folds of the nappy.

The Captain stuttered: 'My God, my God! It *is* a girl, oh the poor, poor creature!'

Then, slowly, he began to laugh and going to his suitcase pulled out the gun and holster, the drum, the drumsticks. He stood there, holding them, and the little boy they were intended for made a low swoop through the air, gave a cheer and a laugh, and disappeared from the world for ever. Nora moved swiftly and flung her arms around the Captain's barrel waist. She loved him, God yes, she loved him, raising her face to his, wanting to be kissed and held so tightly that it would hurt, happy that now they should have a house filled with joy, a young girl tossing her lovely young life around their heavy lives, stitching the three of them into an intimate, unbroken whole.

There was a deep darkness over the island. The shifting winds worked their way through the small pine grove that sheltered the house. The floor of the grove was soft with years of decayed and decaying pine needles. Toadstools grew in small pale groups and moist creeping things worked through the darkness. The night lamp burning in the back bedroom of the house threw a sickly needle of yellow onto the yard towards the wall of the pine grove. The wind shuffled and complained through the trees.

The child slept, Nora at her side. She was aware of the infinite dome of night outside, and beyond the nameable sounds of the wind she knew there stretched the might of the ocean that heaved and fell in the nurturing of its own, other, sea life. She was aware, too, of the black endlessness of space above and beyond all that she knew and all that was knowable, exploding forever into the mysteries of infinity, eternity and God. She remembered the days when she had spread her hand out over her swollen belly, the fingers splayed as if she would protect the growing child within her from the pressures of the universe and from the eyes of God. She sat now, quietened, on the edge of the bed, her body swaying slowly as if in memory of the rocking movement when she had held the child close to her before its sleep.

Outside, beyond the pine grove, moving in the darkness, so dark itself it was invisible against the night, something approached across the soft sucking surfaces of the moor. Its rough breathing sound could not be heard above the sound of the night wind, its bulked, looming shape was lost among the humps and hillocks of the ground. It moved purposefully, flowing like water over the ditch at the far end of the pine grove, and began to make its way over the vegetable earth of the pine floor. Animals saw the creature pass and vanished instantly into their own safe, dark places. The shifting scents of putrefying wood and decaying undergrowth yielded to a heavier odour, old and gangrenous and sour, as if from the very heart of a dying earth. The creature stopped. The child in her cradle did not stir.

From the edge of darkness at the grove wall the creature's eyes watched, unblinking, towards the yellow line of light. The eyes stared, yellow too, wide and moist and concentrated. The creature remained perfectly still, one with the boles of trees and the hulks of bushes, only the reek of its presence moving through the night. It stood, and stared, and waited.

Inside the room Nora heard the far howling of a dog. Her hand reached to touch the wicker presence of the cradle. The child's mouth moved soundlessly in a vaguely sucking way; she was breathing loudly through her nose. She shifted slightly, and settled deeper in her sleep.

Nora felt a coldness beginning round her, somewhere high up along her spine. She wrapped herself more tightly in a rug. The tongue of flame in the lamp stammered a moment and the shadows jittered along the walls. She noticed that the curtains were not tightly closed. She stood up slowly. The sound of the bedsprings protesting startled her. She went to the window. Before drawing the curtains closer she held them and looked out. She could see nothing, nothing but blackness. She shivered. Quickly she drew the curtains closed. She wished, suddenly, that the Captain had stayed home tonight. She listened. Only the wind, defining the angles of the house. But she was cold now, very cold, and the child shifted uneasily in the cradle. She leant over to look.

Patricia's eyes scarcely open yet and unfocused, her head moved slowly towards Nora. Gratefully Nora lifted her, keeping her wrapped in her blankets, and sat back on the bed with her, whispering to her, touching her forehead with her lips. Nora opened her blouse and drew the nipple of her breast to the child's mouth.

Out in the wood the creature shifted. There was no light from the window. A low angry growl grew in intensity. High in the branches of a tree a night bird stirred. And then the creature howled, suddenly, out of its darkness, a long, low single note that could have been the moaning of the wind, but it persisted, rising slowly in its animal pitch toward a piercing human scream; then it broke, suddenly, and stopped.

What Nora heard from her room was a moan, an eerie, almost human cry, pleading, seductive, captivating, and the eager mouth at her breast had stopped its sucking, had paused, as if the infant, too, recognised the sound. Nora's body had gone stiff with terror and a chill passed through her. When the howl ended she looked frenziedly towards the curtains. There was no sound. No stir. And then the tiny mouth was working at her breast again and the eyes were shut in comfort.

It was after midnight when the Captain came back home. He was in his favoured state of near-intoxication, that state where benevolence dominates, when the future is all brightness, when plans and promises are made and everything becomes more than possible. He found his wife and daughter in the darkness of the bedroom, lying together for comfort, sprawled across the big bed. He lit a candle in the hallway and carried it into the room; he lifted a rug from the foot of the bed and laid it carefully over Nora. He noticed that the wick had burned out in the old oil lamp. He put his fingers to his lips and urged the world to ssshhhhh. He lifted the baby and put her back, with infinite gentleness, into her crib.

He crept out of the bedroom and climbed the stairs to the attic room. It was cold up there but he had his overcoat on. He set the candle on the windowsill, took off his shoes and lay down, fully clothed, on the bed, drawing a rug over his knees. He pulled a half-finished flask of whiskey from his pocket, took a draught, sighed with satisfaction, put the bottle down beside the candle on the sill. What a joy, mother and daughter, curled up together in warmth and peace. He lay back on the pillow and closed his eyes. Life was good. He was happy. All was well.

Patricia, as a name, was acceptable to the Captain. He pronounced that it would do and resolved that he would call her Patty. Close enough, that, close enough. He insisted, too, on the name Lenore, for a child should have a real name, a name that, in the saying of it, would roll around the mouth like a smooth sea stone, a name to lift the girl out of the marshlands of the island and raise her spirit to the adventurous possibilities of life.

And then he would add the name Izabel, for the sake of his wealthy sister who lived alone in a large house in the village of Rathmines, a house filled with stuffs and things, antimacassars, lace, oil paintings, fenders and four-poster beds, andirons, porcelain and apostle spoons, a roll-top writing desk, silver and glass and watches and gold, pewter and Chippendale and Chinese plates, glass-fronted cabinets crammed with the most delicate figurines so that you feared to sneeze lest they explode into dust. For so the Captain dreamed of all the things the little house at the crossroads did not possess. Izabel would be pleased; it would cost the poor child nothing. There would be a will . . .

Patricia Lenore Izabel O'Higgins.

Yes!

He would write at once to Izabel and ask her down for the christening. And then all would be well and all would be as well as the world allowed.

Nora cringed, but complied.

Maggie 'Muttons' O'Driscoll, priest's housekeeper, was plump from ankle to neck. Only her feet and ears were small, dainty, even delicate. She spent half an hour every evening with her feet in a basin of scalding water in which she had dissolved some boric powder. She wiggled her toes in the water; she lifted the hem of her skirt over the crags of her knees, rested her fists on her hams and luxuriated. The cares of day and parish drained away into the water, together with the creaks and groans of her heavy flesh. Then she dried her feet, sprinkled them with baby powder, put on her slippers, opened the back door of the presbytery and flung the water into the rhododendron bushes. Using a matchstick and cotton wool she cleaned her ears with Vaseline oil. To maintain her balance in life. To hear the better the music of living. For there was no woman in the world as balanced as Maggie, nor a woman with as acute a sense of hearing. She listened a while at Father Crowe's door; if all was still she tapped gently, murmured good night, collected the mumbled response; so all was well, all manner of thing was well within; she went to her bed where she dreamed the dreams that only angels dream.

On Mondays and Fridays, and on certain Saturdays of the year, Maggie went as far as Casimir Conlon's shop. Maggie knew a fine empathy with Casimir Conlon, a man of a certain girth himself, built like a gate pier, suffering like Maggie from a delicacy in the feet. Casimir's face was round, his large cheeks the red of beetroot soaked in vinegar. Little beads of sweat grew on Casimir's face, gathered in the valley below his Adam's apple, then dribbled down into the undergrowth on his chest. Sometimes Casimir brushed the back of his wrist across his forehead and flicked the mist of sweat droplets onto the great block of wood he worked at. Seasoning the meat. Salting his butcher's table.

Casimir lived with his mother who, for reasons lost in the past, was known to the world as 'Pee-Wee'. By now she was in her eighties and spent her days and nights 'in the room beyant', a bedroom at the back of Conlon's shop, down a windowless hallway, through a door painted cowpat brown. There she lived in the hot and crowded village of her bed, shrunken and wizened and bitter, filling her bulging missal with memoriam cards, gloating over each added name and face, then repenting by praying the prayers and harvesting the indulgences specified on each card.

Maggie passed the open door of Conlon's shed, better known as the 'slaughterhouse'. There was a sheep hanging by its hocks, blood was dripping, plop, plop, plip-plop, into a white enamel bath. The carcass turned slowly, reached the tension of the rope that held it, paused, then began to turn slowly in the other direction. For a moment Maggie watched it, held in awe before the laws of nature. On a bench at the side of the shed were Casimir's tools of trade, knives, shears, hacksaw, ropes. Maggie shuddered. Plop, plink, plip-ploppppppop. Still, she thought, people's got to live and even Father enjoys his puddings.

The door of the shop opened into a large cold room, facing north, lit always by one naked bulb. From the ceiling hung coils of greasy brown flypaper dotted with corpses. For counter Casimir used an enormous block of wood mounted on thick wooden legs. Over the years, this block had been hollowed in the centre and had grown soft from blood and scalding water, and rough from the hacking, sawing, slicing it had suffered. Behind Casimir, against the wall, was a deal table covered with a blue-and-white-squared oil-cloth. Here, on trays, he displayed the meats he had prepared, the chops, the necks, the livers, the hearts . . .

'Ah ha, Maggie!' he roared. 'Is it yourself is in it?'

'Mr Conlon, how are you today? And how is poor old Pee-Wee?'

'Grand, grand, grand! Not a bother on her at all. Beyant prayin', as usual, though she got a quare shkelp of a frekken th'other night made her double her prayers, the poor bashte.'

'A frekken, Mr Conlon? What class of a frekken?'

Casimir leant conspiratorially over his chopping board, the congealed blood on his dirty apron rubbing gently on the flesh of the lamb he was carving. (Maggie always soaked Casimir's meats in cold salted water before she cooked them.)

'Banshee,' he whispered. 'Banshee. Heard it ourselves both. No doubt about it, no doubt at all.'

'Oh go on with you, Casimir! If you'd just come to church like everybody else, you'd know that that's all pure superstition.'

'Ssshhhh,' he whispered, his finger to his lips, his eyes towards the brown door. '*She* does think that I do go, it gives me a few hours' peace of a Sunday. Herself heard it beyant in the room and if she was fit enough she'd be hangin' out o' th'altar rails till Father Crowe himself couldn't shift her, she got that much of a frekken. She knows, you see, she knows 'twas the banshee she heard and nothin' else. An' her as good a Chrisken as ever was. There's for you. An' me, I heard it, an' I'm no soft daub for anyone to leave their shoe print on. No queskin about it. No queskin. There now, Maggie, there's for you.'

There came a piercing high-pitched screech from the room beyant. Maggie jumped. She could not understand a syllable out of that awful cry.

But Casimir, his eyes rolling towards the ceiling, roared back: 'Only Father Crowe's Maggie, Mum, 'tis only Father Crowe's Maggie.'

'I'll take four of your best cutlets, Casimir, a nice piece of neck and some chops. I'll make Father the very best of Irish stews.'

Casimir busied himself at the table. 'A wailin' sound, Maggie, in the middle of the night, these few nights back, a long low wail, risin' risin' risin' to a howl then droppin' droppin' droppin' back to a wail' – Casimir's voice rose and fell dramatically in the telling – 'that kept on like you'd hear the wind in between gusts, then off again, wail, howl, wail, an' all of it'd put the hair on your chest rigid as a barbed-wire fence. If you'll pardon the expression, Maggie. I have the loveliest shoulder of mutton here now I'm sure the devil himself would give his horns for, never mind Father Crowe, who's certain sure to be shlaverin' like a wolf over it.'

'Just your best end neck, Mr Conlon, please, an' you can throw in a nice bit of liver for myself. A bit of drippin', too, that's a good man.'

The piercing shriek came again from the room beyant. Again Maggie could not decipher a word.

'Sounds a bit like the banshee herself, Casimir, if you don't take offence.'

'Indeed no offence, Maggie, sure you know what I have to go through with her. Th'oul' crusht! She has me heart an' me liver scalded out o' me. Hold on there a minute, Maggie, her kidneys is at her again. I'll have to lift her in the bed. I'll be shtraight back to parcel you up your shtuff.'

Rubbing his hands on his apron, Casimir headed down the hallway towards the brown door. Maggie shuddered. There was a thin filament of black blood moving over the hacked slope of the butcher's board. Where it fell on the concrete floor beneath to form a pool, there was a fat black beetle taking its pleasure. Maggie hurried to the door and looked out over the fields towards the sea, trying to distract her mind from what was happening in the room beyant.

She could see the house of the Captain and Nora O'Higgins, the small grove of pine trees that formed a sheltering belt to the northern side, the rough track that led up through the meadows to the lake. Away over the ditches and fields, the low hills covered in ferns and gorse, she could see the village with its tiny harbour; the sea, from where she stood, looked calm and beautiful. Clean. Pure. Beyond that, the plum-and-raisin-coloured mountains of the mainland.

She heard Casimir reopen the door; he came out holding a shallow basin, passed through his shop and went out a side door. Maggie heard a slooshing of water from the tap at the side of the slaughterhouse. She heard Casimir pass back through the shop, and she could hear muttering and whining from the room beyant. The brown door closed again. Maggie coughed delicately into her fist and faced back into the shop. Casimir was wiping his hands on his apron.

'She wants to know, Maggie, who was it died in the last two or three days?'

'There's nobody at all 'as died, Mr Conlon, only there's a new life come into the world at the Captain's place. Nora Corrigan has given birth to a grand wee girl. There's for you and your banshee.'

Casimir stood, gaping. 'Well, the poor child, that's all I can say,' he muttered. 'The poor child, born into the wail of the banshee. You know, Maggie' – as he stooped back over the meat – 'I have no bother at all in heftin' a Black-faced Scotch from the floor to the ceilin' but Mum above, and her no bigger than a sheep's shit, I almost break my back to hoist her off her arse!'

'Mr Conlon, please! My ears, man, my ears. You'll burn them, man, you'll set them afire. This Scotch now, that would be a whiskey, would it not?'

'Ah Maggie, that's what comes of truckin' with God an' priests, you don't know fat from drippin'. The Black-faced Scotch is your sheep. Like the Cheviot, the Welsh, the Kerry. The Black-face has horns, her hair is like Mum's beyant, she's a bit wild like her too, an' so she doesn't fatten up that good. There now.' He slapped her order onto a brown paper sheet, rolled it up, wrapped it round and tied it with a length of twine. 'Food for himself an' yourself an' I suppose it goes on the Pope's bill, as usual.'

'Good man, Mr Conlon. And if you came to church on Sundays and Holy Days and maybe came to Benediction once or twice and made your peace with God above, your own mother would be happy and your sacred soul' – Maggie's eyes wandered quickly round the shop – 'would be pure and clean and shining and the banshee and all the things you believe to be living inside your darkness would have no more power over you than the wind.'

Maggie was a great ball of dignity as she left, the brown paper package gripped under one arm. Casimir Conlon watched her as she left, trying to imagine the size and shape of those buttocks and how she'd be if she stood naked. He grinned a huge grin; poor Muttons, he thought, poor Muttons O'Driscoll, she'll never get a man, what with a body like that an' the priesht havin' his eye on her every turn. Poor Maggie Muttons, poor solitary soul, and he wiped a great line of sweat from his forehead and sprinkled it over his chopping board.

Izabel Ingrid O'Higgins liked nothing more than to create a fuss about her person. Some three days before the christening of baby Izabel she took the train to Westport but was unable to get any further. There was no train connection for the island. She refused to travel by bus; such a crush, she would say, such a rickety old machine, such fumes, such sweaty characters about her, and then she could never be sure where exactly she would have to get off. On top of all of that she always felt somewhat ill before the colour green and the bus – my God where did they get that shade of green? Gone-off cabbage, that's what it was, a gone-off-cabbage green.

The Captain suffered a telegram. 'STRANDED WESTPORT STOP PLEASE RESCUE STOP IZABEL STOP.'

The address was given as the Railway Hotel. It was evening. The Captain's temper was stretched. He cycled as far as Larry-the-Reek's store. He promised a generous fee. Pat's van was taken out and they set off.

It was after ten when they arrived at the Railway Hotel. Izabel was sitting alone in the lounge, surrounded by drumlins of baggages. She had been fortifying herself on sweet sherries and was, for once, in a giggly mood.

'Cyril, darling!' she greeted her brother, and tried to embrace him. Her knees hit the low table before her and the sherry glass tumbled. She sat back heavily in her chair. 'Oops!' she said, putting one hand to her powdered face and laughing towards Pat. 'Oh dear, I've pooped!'

Pat Larry didn't know what to do with his hands and his eyes had taken to roving rapidly all over the lounge without being able to focus on anything. Then he discovered Izabel's trunk and suitcases and his worries were over. 'These yours, ma'am?' Without waiting for a reply he began to haul them out to the van.

The Captain took the muttering Izabel by one arm and led her out after much fumbling and fussing to see she had not forgotten anything. Soon they were on the road for home, Izabel asleep and propped on the same sacks that Nora had used some time earlier, while the Captain and Pat Larry talked quietly through the thickening night.

Izabel was small, pinched and shrewish-looking. Her fur coat hung largely about her, her high-heeled shoes lay on the floor of the van like small beached boats. She breathed unevenly, twitching in her sleep like a dreaming cat.

'Izabel will have to be forgiven a great deal,' the Captain was saying out of his sudden benevolence. 'Her life, Pat, has been far from smooth.'

Izabel had been beautiful but she had locked her beauty away behind an all-pervasive haughtiness. Beauty is a gift, the Captain explained, it is not earned, Pat, and it should be shared freely about. She had been bright, too, and men are afraid of a beautiful woman who is both bright and haughty. She had developed a contempt for all things male and that extended gradually to all her women friends who were foolish enough even to look at a man.

By the time she was twenty-one Izabel had closed off most of her options. She spent her days at home, reading and brooding, disdaining housework, gun club dances, socials, beach parties, and she withered any young man who happened to step under the searing glare of her wondrous eyes. She had a bath every day in the days when a bath was filled only by dint of boiling up large black kettles of lake water on the stove. She studied make-up – creams, lotions, unguents, both artificial and natural – she studied the newspaper advertisements and talked on and on about all the new potions, lotions and notions announced for the preservation of everlasting youth and beauty.

'To what purpose, Pat?' asked the Captain. 'To what purpose? She would not let love in, every chink and keyhole was boarded up. Love, Pat, love, that is what Izabel could never, ever know.'

Izabel Ingrid O'Higgins, he opined, tossed her curls at the world, held her lovely body erect and withdrew into the sweet and remote dream of herself.

'What a shock, then, Pat, what a mystery, when Izabel announced, in the spring of '41, that she was for England to volunteer as a nurse with the services. And that was that. She said no more, offered no explanations, listened to no remonstrances, but packed her toiletries and disappeared into the maelstrom of the war. No card, no note, no telegram ever came; it was as if she had no friends nor acquaintances on this earth, Pat, and nobody ever heard word of her, nor did we know for years if she was alive or dead.'

But here she was, old long before her time, as if the years she had hoped to parry had rushed the more heavily upon her; she was wizened, cranky, drunk, delivered from Rathmines via Westport and Pat Larry's van, and lodged in the attic room of the Captain's house. This room was comfortable, quaint, with a view over fields to the sea. For Izabel would not sleep on the ground floor, not under any circumstances. She would stiffen into a trance of agony at the mere possibility of cockroaches, those marauders that came out at night and worked their way silently about the floor. Up to God alone knew what mischief and carrying God alone knew what awful diseases. Even upstairs, in her attic room, she sprinkled the bedroom floor with DDT, around the skirting boards, around the legs of chairs and the legs of the bed, the white strong-smelling powder constituting a bunker wherein she could maintain her defences.

Izabel spent her mornings indoors, withdrawn, her afternoons pottering about in the small parlour, disappearing at intervals to change her clothes, to sit in the window alcove gazing down towards the sea. She paid no attention to the baby girl whose timely popping in out of the darkness of eternity had been the source of Izabel's invitation to visit. She hummed to herself perpetually as she floated from place to place, a lace handkerchief in her right hand carried often to her nose and mouth. She hummed tunes, the Captain supposed, popular in the years she had been afloat on the raft of her dreams; but by now – the way marl in all its colours and smoothness eventually blends into a dull grey mess – there was no trace left of recognisable tune, rhythm or melody. Izabel sighed and gazed away from the world into the blank face of time.

3

I f she could get far enough away before they missed her they might not catch her and bring her back. In the distance the streetlights of the town cast a faint, dull but warm glow against the sky. There were trees. She sensed rather than saw the road. She had to walk slowly. Her feet, through the thin slippers and goloshes, could feel the rough stone edge of the road; beyond that there was a margin of grass. She moved, feeling for the gravel edge and the grass, unknowing whether there was a drain or a fence or a field beyond. She was cold. She waved her arms about and tried to walk more rapidly. She grew breathless. She had to stop, bending forward, her hands on her knees, inhaling, exhaling . . .

'Stay calm, now, calm, above all be calm, calm, calm.'

She spoke the words into the darkness and they fell about her feet, skittering away from her like startled beetles. She moved again, admitting the cold, allowing the weariness to invade her mind, going slowly, slowly, but with a steady impetus.

Only once, in that interminable period of darkness, did a vehicle go past. It had come towards her, heading for the town. It did not scare her; she knew its name, *car*, she could handle it. First the lights, a shifting white vagueness in the distance like a ghost moving among the hills. Then the two white beams. They appeared and fell away again, beyond a hill, beyond trees. And suddenly it was upon her, looming round a corner as if it had been waiting to pounce. She could distinguish nothing in the sudden glare. She raised one hand to shield her eyes from the light. The car slowed momentarily, she heard the engine falter, she knew she must be a spectre at that strange hour. The car cruised past her, the driver, on whatever errand, having made a decision about her. She watched the red tail lights, saw how the main beams lit up the trees, the bushes, the road, and then the car was gone, leaving around her a stronger sense of loneliness and silence, a more acute awareness of her own strained breathing. The driver would remember a spirit, a lost soul, shifting through the middle kingdom.

She seemed to struggle on for hours and still the daylight did not come. She stopped often, to rest, nervous of proximity to drain or ditch, cautious of how the road veered and tilted as if it too was urgent to fling her off its back. When at last the first faint warning of day appeared on the horizon she knew she was heading in the right direction. Westward. Towards home. And freedom.

Light began to glimmer on the surface of a wide water. She noticed it first as a faint gleam, a suggestion, almost a memory of light. And then she heard it – the sleepy pattering of water against a shore. There would be rocks. Bushes. Shelter. She could rest.

Almost before she knew it another car had topped the horizon and was bearing suddenly towards her. She was aware, at once, of the ugly blue light turning silently on its roof. The headlights, too, looked menacing in the beginning of dawn. She cried out in terror and rushed into whatever darkness waited to the side. She fell, scrabbling wildly for hold, down a shingle embankment, feeling the harsh surface scrape at her body; she came to a stop on soft growth, grass, or moss, or ferns, and the dampness immediately touched her, cold and clammy against her skin. Her wrist was hurting, fear hammered in her heart. She lay still.

The car passed slowly along the road above her. She knew it was the enemy, watchful, hunting, she knew the beam of its blue eye striking the world about her. She would lose her mind under their vengeful punishings. She lay still. As if dead. Silence settled back; she could hear the bubbling of ditch water about her. She lay on. Sobbing. How the heart in its hiding stirs for peace, for release from the beasts that plague it. How good it would be to melt away, like water into water, like breath into air. The coldness hurt. She slipped and slithered up out of the ditch, the hospital overalls clinging against her, impeding her. She came on to the road. There was no light visible. The enemy had been foiled. Once again. But for the moment only.

She could distinguish now, on the other side of the road, the looming shape of a house, long and low, under the pre-dawn light. At her back, the lake. She crossed the road, moving along the shingle as quietly as she could. She reached a gate pier, there was a cattle grid, she passed over it onto a driveway. There were bushes, shrubs; a car was waiting outside a garage door; the bungalow was like a coffin in the darkness, big and daunting and still as death. She moved around the side of the garage. The gravel seemed to hiss and spit under her feet. If there were a dog now . . .

Her God was with her. There was a shed. Across the space behind the house, a clothesline. Jeans. Underwear. A blouse. A towel. Other things, gatherings for the living and the whole. Cautiously she lifted down what she would need. They were damp. The little heat left in her blood would dry them. And did it matter anyway? Gingerly she drew back the bolt on the shed door. It squealed once and she froze. Perhaps, through someone's dream in the sleeping house, a wild bird screeched in the distance. She felt no guilt. She was in need, her life depending. She found a pair of wellingtons. There was a fisherman's coat on the wall and another smaller one, plastic, with a hood. She took the smaller coat and the wellingtons and left. The brightness of a day of freedom would soon spread over the land.

At the lake's edge she washed, her white and naked body little more than a ghost materialising out of the dawn mist. The water was cold, clear, refreshing; she towelled herself as dry as she could and dressed in the borrowed clothes. The clothes were a child's clothes but she too was small, smaller and thinner now than many children. Clumps of sallies and ghostly bushes of fuchsia stood on guard around her, dull and unspeaking as those with whom she had shared a ward. As the light grew she sat on a rock and watched the gentle waters of the lake. Her face peered back at her. A lily. Vulnerable.

Narcissus, she whispered to herself, and smiled. About her, thin congregations of slender reeds stood in the shallow water, making a faint, plaintive sound. Narcissus; she said it aloud to the reeds and they whispered the name back to her. Echo, she said. Narcissus, they whispered back. I would be glad to make such music for ever, she thought, relishing the soft silver presences. She looked about her, along the lake shore, back to where she could see the roof of the bungalow emerge over the bushes, kindly now in the gathering light. She reached and drew her hand gently up the long smooth stem of a reed. Her fingers held, for a moment, the soft velvety tip. 'You and I will always talk together so,' she whispered. The reed swayed. She gathered the red plastic raincoat about her and turned, still shivering, back towards the road.

4

Casimir Conlon came out of the room beyant and banged the door behind him. His mother had been insisting again that Casimir court Maggie O'Driscoll before he grew to be as useless as a cart without shafts.

'Walk out with her for a few years,' the old woman whined from the hot wilderness of her bed. 'Take her out to the lake, take her up the hills on walks, go to a dance, go to a ceilidh, something. But walk her out! Then when I'm gone you can marry her and bring her in here. But not till I'm gone, mind. I couldn't have her likes in here gawking and poking at me and me on my bed of pain.'

Casimir stomped out the side door of the shop into his yard. Marry Maggie indeed. He knew he was no Clark Gable himself but he deserved more in life than a Maggie Muttons O'Driscoll. Oh yes, she had flesh, yes, like a Tamworth pig, round and smooth and pink-coloured. And no doubt the flesh would taste like the flesh of a Tamworth pig, and handle so as well. Casimir Conlon was a hearty heft of a man and would be so these forty years to come. He had time, time to wait for a delicate white-fleshed girl who would relish his experience and his strength. If that's all his mother thought of him then she could go shite in her own bed.

Instantly Casimir regretted the thought. And at that very moment he saw the door of his slaughterhouse wide open. He remembered closing it, barely ten minutes ago, just before he had gone in to see to Pee-Wee's needs. This morning he had slaughtered a special sheep, his very first large Roscommon, refined by crossing with a Leicester. He was delighted with the result, a fine-quality sheep that was able to take the winds and famine grasses of the mountainside. And from the day before, he had a Black-faced Scotch hanging from his roof beams, ready now to be brought in for carving. He looked in the door of the shed. Both of his sheep were gone.

His first thought was that God was punishing him for his dream of finding a fine-fleshed young woman with whom he could mate and for insulting and then ignoring the housekeeper of a servant of God. Then he cursed himself for the thought: he did not believe in God. Some of the local wasters must have carted off his sheep.

There was a thin trail of blood leading across the yard towards the fence. The whures must have hauled the bashtes over the fence. How could they have done that? The fence did not appear to be damaged. Here and there, like tufts of the bog cotton, clumps of white and off-white wool were caught. He whistled up his dog, Fluther, from his sleeping place on a sack inside the back door of the house and made him sniff the blood along the yard. Then Casimir climbed laboriously over the fence and Fluther started off across the common ground towards the boglands and the low hills before the mountain. They couldn't get far across this terrain, Casimir muttered and spat viciously onto the ground. He could find drops of blood along the hummocks of grass and heather. The dog was moving swiftly on the trail. Casimir expected him to swerve back at any moment towards the village but the dog was heading in a straight line for the hills.

Casimir was puzzled; how could they haul, and so quickly, his two days' work along with them. There were deep marks in the soft ground, they could be the prints of boots, they could be the marks of dragged or dangled animals. They came to the more stony ground of the hillside. The dog did not hesitate in his excited rush. Fluther was growling and barking soft sharp yelps, snout low along the earth, tail taut. Casimir cursed and snorted in his efforts to keep up.

Soon a small stone hut that had been used years ago by shrimp fishermen appeared above him. It was a stone shell, one gable wall completely gone, the other facing inland, retaining the rough shape of what had been a window. The side walls had collapsed. The stones lay scattered, losing themselves in the grasses and heathers. It was a sheltering place for sheep on the lower slopes of the mountain. The dog disappeared, growling, around the angle of the wall. Casimir stooped and gathered a rock into his fist; he waited for the snarl of the dog, expecting to see his quarry come bolting out of their hiding place. Christ! He'd lave welts on their hides and mangle the worth of the flesh out of their stinkin' corpses!

When he reached the hut there was only chaos. The dog was nosing around the outer edges of the ruin. There were traces of wool and blood on the trodden earthen floor as if the sheep had been torn into pieces and devoured on this very spot. Tiny gobbets of red flesh were scattered about. There was one skull, naked to the bone, bits of gristle and wool attached, but what terrified Casimir most was that the skull itself had been broken in two, as if by the force of irresistible jaws. Casimir shuddered, his big frame ready to melt with anger before this destruction of his property, to flow with fear before the fury of the carnage.

He looked up the slopes of the mountain over the broken wall; there was only the wind and the shivering naked slopes. He gazed on the hard earth again, looking for footprints. There were many confused marks, a slithering, hurrying mess. Could it have been a pack of dogs? He would have heard them bark, they would have left a great deal more rag and gristle of their prey all over the mountainside. Here there was little solid enough for his mind to gather.

He began to move, hesitantly, further up the flanks of the mountain. The rage was quickly dripping out of him, giving place to doubt and caution. He was all alone up here, and something fierce and aggressive was up here with him.

Casimir felt a wave of cold flood over his body. Fluther was watching him, alert and waiting. All around and above there was only the bleak space of a mindless landscape stretching into the higher reaches of the mountain. Casimir turned quickly, half-expecting to find something dreadful waiting to strike him down. There was nothing. The dog yelped, startled by the sudden movement.

The big man found himself muttering, 'Jesus! Jesus! Jesus!' and deep down in his soul he admitted it was a prayer. For some moments he stood petrified as a bog-oak root. He knew the hair on the back of his neck had begun to bristle. He watched the dog who stood, indifferent now, as if it all had been merely a sudden interesting game. From the dog's indifference he gained some courage. Quickly he began to make his way back down towards his home.

In 1941, Izabel Ingrid O'Higgins had presented herself to the authorities in London. She became a nurse and served in France and Italy. She was on board ship in the Mediterranean when it was torpedoed and almost everybody killed. She spent days in the water with only the tyre of a jeep to keep her afloat. She worked for the remainder of the war in tent hospitals in North Africa. There she saw it all, the agony and distress that man can work on man, the torn limbs and smashed-in faces, the wrecked bones, the exploded minds – but she worked tirelessly and without complaint across those awful years.

It was because of her aunt that Patricia Lenore Izabel O'Higgins arrived late for her own christening. Father Crowe had waited patiently for a time, pacing up and down the sacristy floor, then going outside and circling the church several times. He had gone back to the presbytery, leaving instructions that, should they arrive within the next hour, they could send for him. After that, he had a game of golf to play with Doctor Weir – and he couldn't keep the good doctor waiting for him on the windy edge of the links.

Izabel had been wholly unable to fasten her waif-like body into the red dress she had brought with her for the occasion. Nora, summoned upstairs, had failed to see anything wrong with dress or fit and was quickly dismissed while Izabel regrouped herself, slowly, into her travelling clothes. Patricia Lenore Izabel slept peacefully. The Captain, in a panic, finally shouted up the stairs that they were leaving at once and she had bloody well bundle herself into some old flounces of cotton or wool and not be making a production of herself before the whole countryside. This outburst brought on a major attack of frigidity in poor Izabel who, when she did deign to speak to the Captain again, declared herself mortified by the ignorance and obtuseness of the island peasantry as a whole. She was delivered to the station late that afternoon, allowing herself the in-between hours to gather herself into portable shape. Not one word would she address to Pat Larry on the road in spite of his faltering attempts to dunt the iceberg of her presence. At the station, however, she paid him well for the journey and gave him an extra gift of five shillings – for his courtesy and consideration, she murmured from her great, great height.

For years afterwards Izabel Ingrid O'Higgins never wrote or spoke to her brother, the Captain, except when, once a year, she telephoned and insisted on speaking to little Izabel and to her alone.

'Is that the house of Mr and Mrs O'Higgins?'

'Yes, this is Cyril speaking.'

'May I speak with Baby Izabel, please?'

'Is that you, Izabel? Lovely to hear from you. How are you at all, at all?'

'Is Baby Izabel there, please? I wish to speak with her.'

'Hold on a moment, then. Patty's six now. I'll get her for you.'

And that was that. Patty kept in touch with her aunt, sending letters on fancy paper with coloured envelopes that had bunnies, teddies, baby elephants printed on them. The only acknowledgement was the yearly phone call, sometimes close to Christmas, never predictable.

'How are you, Izabel?'

'Hello, Auntie Izabel. I'm very well, thank you, how are you?'

'Thank you, Izabel, for your letters and postcards.'

'Oh you're welcome. Did you ever ... ?'

'I'm sending you something for yourself, Izabel. You must write and let me know that it has arrived safely. Will you do that?'

'Of course I will, Auntie. You're very kind. But you mustn't bother, truly you …'

'Very well, Izabel. Goodbye now.'

No package ever did arrive from Auntie Izabel and so no acknowledgement could ever be written. For years the young girl imagined boxes and parcels wrapped in delightfully striped and dia-monded colours, tied about with yellow and blue twine, all piled up in a post office or a railway station somewhere between the island and the capital, mouldering away in some small town.

There was a small gathering in the O'Higgins house on the eve-ning of the christening, the Captain swelling to his role of father, master again of his castle after the dismissal, as he called it, of his spoiled and self-centred sister. He expanded on the names he had chosen for his lovely daughter and recited, in a dramatic, sonorous voice, the poem by Edgar Allan Poe that had inspired him:

Ah, broken is the golden bowl! the spirit flown forever!
Let the bell toll! – a saintly soul floats on the Stygian river;
And, Guy de Vere, hast *thou* no tear? – weep now or never more!
See! on yon drear and rigid bier low lies thy love, Lenore!
Come! let the burial rite be read – the funeral song be sung!
An anthem for the queenliest dead that ever died so young.
A dirge for the doubly dead in that she died so young.

From her corner where she sat in the room, Nora could be heard muttering during this performance. But the Captain ignored her, relishing his position, standing with a glass of whiskey in his right hand, his left elbow elegantly and poetically resting on the high mantelpiece behind him.

Wretches! ye loved her for her wealth and hated her for her pride,
And when she fell in feeble health, ye blessed her – that she died!
How *shall* the ritual then be read? the requiem how be sung
By you – by yours, the evil eye – by yours, the slanderous tongue
That did to death the innocent that died, and died so young?

The Captain paused, made a mournful face, shook his handsome head and, to seal the moment, took a slow sip from his whiskey.

Peccavimus; but rave not thus! and let a Sabbath song
Go up to God so solemnly the dead may feel no wrong!
The sweet Lenore hath 'gone before' with Hope, that flew beside,

Leaving thee wild for the dear child that should have been thy bride –
For her, the fair and *debonair*, that now so lowly lies,
The life upon her yellow hair but not within her eyes –
The life still there, upon her hair – the death upon her eyes.

Again Nora's muttering voice could be heard, words like *miserable* and *black* and *depressing* and *pessimistic* – but the Captain was leading up to his favourite word and nothing could stop the waterfall of his performance.

'Avaunt!' The Captain paused. Smiled. Began again.

Avaunt! to-night my heart is light. No dirge will I upraise,
But waft the angel on her flight with a Paean of old days!
Let *no* bell toll! – lest her sweet soul, amid its hallowed mirth
Should catch the note, as it doth float – up from the damnèd Earth.
To friends above, from fiends below, the indignant ghost is riven –
From Hell unto a high estate far up within the Heaven –
From grief and groan, to a golden throne, beside the King of Heaven.

The last verses were a peroration, the Captain stepping away from the fireplace onto the centre of the rug, raising both hands towards the ceiling, spilling a small mist of golden liquid onto the floor at his feet, and then bowing low as the last lines fell melodiously from his lips. During the applause he smiled towards them all and lifted his glass once again, to the health, long life and happiness of his daughter, Patricia Lenore Izabel.

Together Father Crowe and Doctor Weir began to climb up the valley. There had been talk, rumours, anxieties. The priest was still optimistic and fervent, the doctor wholehearted and generous. The day was a fair one, the sky barely touched by clouds, the breeze refreshing in the heat of the climb. Beneath them they could see the clear, sheltered waters of a bay, a few currachs out on the water, hunting the basking shark. The long cleft of the valley was moist and fragrant. They strode out with pleasure.

'Evil's been with us since Adam, Jim,' the priest was saying.

Father Crowe was a big man, his black hair combed like a child's, his jaw strong and determined against the things of Satan. 'The flaw is deep within us, ineradicable. Evil's in our nature, man, and only the hand of God Himself can root it out. That's what Christ's death was all about. That's what Christ living on in the Church is all about.'

The doctor laboured on beside him, thoughtfully. They passed an old coastguard station, already falling into ruin before the onslaughts of Atlantic storms. They jumped a small stream. The doctor was small, ascetic-looking, jerky in his actions as if he were impatient with the passing of time. His thin fair hair blew in strands over his bright, intent face. They were both sweating already in the warmth of the afternoon.

Father Crowe paused and leant his right hand on a large rock. 'Penal altar, Jim,' he commented, 'used down the centuries as a secret place for saying Masses. What a perfect hideaway, this valley, almost inaccessible by land in those years. The people flocked here in their hundreds by currach, or struggling over these slopes. Wonderful years of faith. Our faith has always flourished in times of persecution.'

'Faith!' the doctor said. 'I only wish I had a faith like that. It's my belief that the whole weight of the past presses down on us, Donal, all that weight of wars and persecutions, the screams of despair and agony down all the years. It hangs on the air like a pestilence. Thickening with every century as generation after generation adds its own horrors to the great sum of horror of which man has been guilty. A miasma. This thing of Adam makes it all too easy. Not our fault. Adam's fault. Too easy, far too easy.'

Father Crowe laughed. 'On a lovely afternoon like this, it's hard to think of the air filled with wickedness. Look at the clarity of the sky, the beauty of the heather, a cloudless day.'

The doctor turned and faced back down the valley towards the bay. He could see a great distance out over the sea, across a shimmering ocean, over islands and cliffs to Croagh Patrick and the mountains of Connemara. The world shimmered in a silvery beauty. He chuckled. 'Let's get on with this climb, and save our breath to feed our ardour.'

They topped the valley and entered on a flat area of moist peatland. They stepped carefully, afraid the ground, soft and wet, would suck them in. They walked a while in silence.

The doctor stopped suddenly. Then he said : 'Have you noticed there isn't a sheep in sight. We have not seen one sheep since we set out.'

The priest paused. He gazed around the slopes. There was no movement. Not a sign of life. 'Yes, it's peculiar,' he agreed. 'Perhaps they've all taken their sheep down to the village fields, scared to think what has been happening up in the pastures. Maybe your miasma of evil hangs over this old valley, Jim. It would make you wonder, right enough. As if there were a presence here, hostile, threatening. Alien.'

'Come on, let's face into the real climb before we get too scared and turn back. According to you, though, we're carrying that evil with us, so we can't escape it anyway.'

'There's always the power of the exorcism,' the priest commented. 'I've studied it well, Jim, and it fascinates me. The priest, if he's pure enough, can call on the very power of God Himself to enter him, and then he can channel that power towards the poor suffering soul and rid that soul of the evil that has invaded it. It's our way of continuing the divine intervention in the affairs of men. It's a wonderful thing, a great grace, but a rare one.'

'I believe in medicine, Donal, medicine. You can take most illnesses now and treat them, operate, prescribe, heal. Whenever I get stuck I promise to come to you and prescribe your exorcism for my patients.'

They were climbing along the edge of the high cliffs that lead suddenly and precipitately high into the reaches of the mountain. Below them they saw the wild lashes of the ocean against the rocks even though the day was calm. With each step they rose higher and higher, both men falling silent under the effort of the climb. The view out over the ocean was spectacular, the haughtiness of the cliff faces disconcerting. They paused often, catching breath.

Doctor Weir pointed out a great wound in the face of the cliffs below them and to their right. 'Looks like a great landslide or a kind of explosion. Maybe that talk about a plane during the war had some glimmer of truth behind it after all. And all the slippage has formed a kind of island down in the sea below. Look.'

Far below the waves crashed against the rocks and clay of the fall. The sun gleamed beautifully off the breaking, shifting waters.

There was not a gull, nor chough, nor fulmar to be seen or heard. The silence that weighed so heavily under the sounds of the wind and the ocean began to hurt them.

'I have a very strong sense of oppression on me, Jim. Even a sort of anger that seems to have settled on me out of the air. I don't know what it is. Everything is so empty, so full of foreboding.'

The doctor nodded, slowly. He looked at the priest. Then he looked quickly about the slopes above them and across the face of the cliffs below. He frowned and stood up abruptly. 'I feel it too, Donal. A sort of fury rising in me, without focus. You feel as if you might do something disastrous, for no reason. It's real, yet it's wholly intangible –'

He broke off suddenly. Near them and to the right there came a fall of shale down the cliff face, as if something had shifted. They stiffened. They heard the small clattering sound of the clay and stones.

The doctor reached his hand towards the priest. 'Let's get the hell out of here,' he whispered.

Father Crowe began to climb along the cliff edge a little higher, towards the place where they had seen the fall. 'It's some animal or other, that's all. A goat, or a sheep . . .'

He came over the small ledge that had hidden their view of the terrain further on. There was nothing. Cliffs and slopes stretched away, silent, beautiful and still as death. He felt cold. He turned towards the doctor. His face was grim. 'I should pray, Jim, I should do something here to drive away whatever evil exists, but I feel wholly incapable of prayer, as if something had stood suddenly between me and the sun, between me and what I believe in.'

The doctor forced a laugh. 'You know what, Donal? I think we're both growing just a little crazy up here. Perhaps some other day we can climb back up to this spot from the other direction, cover the whole cliff that way, and the mountain reaches. Perhaps we could come back again, armed. But for God's sake let's go. Now.'

He began to climb back down the cliff edge, hurrying, scarcely waiting to see if the priest were following. Father Crowe hesitated a moment longer. He looked out over the whole vast emptiness of the mountain slopes. There was something. Of that he was certain.

He knew that some eyes were watching him. With malevolence. He shivered. Then he turned to follow his friend back down to the floor of the world.

As she grew older, Patty shifted her life further and further back from the dark company of her mother. She left the back yard of the house and followed a cart track up past the vegetable garden, past the turf banks, as far as the lake. There was a corner where the Captain's land ended and that of their neighbours began; a ragged barbed-wire fencing with concrete posts erected on rocks ran out about three yards into the lake, creating a miniature harbour, sheltered and warm. Patty sat on one of the fallen rocks and plopped stones into the lake. A clump of tall reeds grew together out in the water and swayed and shifted delicately. Nearer to where she sat, water grasses grew in the shallows and trailed their long green arms over the surface of the lake. She gazed abstractedly across the lake towards the brown and purple wastes of the hills that rose away from the far bank, ridged and pretty and barren. It was a desolate, treeless landscape but she relished it.

She sat quietly, absorbed in the landscape, becoming almost a part of it. She glanced up once and there was a fox watching her; he stood alert, his whole body in its soft orange colouring turned to her presence, the tail, soft and flimsy as a breath, stretched behind him, right forepaw raised, and held. For a long moment they watched one another, his big brown eyes unblinking, her heart beating faster with delight. She scarcely breathed, at one with his caution, his silence, his challenging brightness, at one for a moment with his life among the humps and hollows of the heathland.

She seemed to sense something else from him, something from his very stance and silence, as if he had spoken to her across the great divide of their separate existences. A whisper, an admonition, offered out of friendship and caring. Words unvoiced, a voice unworded. Something about caution before the world, about concern, something too about pain, about distant places where suffering is borne in secret, endured without sound, among the dripping

54

of the water from heather roots, among fragrances of damp turf banks and fern fronds. Something about carrying your wounds into the easing darkness of a cave underground. Then, just as unexpectedly, the fox moved on again, unhurriedly, without a sound, crossing over the bank and through scutch grasses, moving the way water flows into the untutored boglands beyond her. She sighed, contentedly, and smiled to herself.

'Animals can talk, Mamsa, can't they?'

Nora was sitting at the big window, hands idling in her lap. 'Only in stories, pet.'

'Like the wolf in the story of Red Riding Hood?'

'Like the wolf.'

'But can't other animals talk? The fox, for instance?'

'No, pet, only in stories. Animals can't talk.'

'And are the stories true, Mamsa?'

Nora turned to look at her daughter. Sometimes still her heart lifted when she held her. Sometimes still the sheer innocence and openness of the child sang aloud to the woman. Nora reached out quickly and drew the girl to her, crushing her against her breasts, seeking comfort, some small reassurance. Patty gasped.

'Oh sorry, darling, Mamsa didn't mean to hurt you. It's just – I love you so much, so very, very much.'

Patty pursed her lips and reached her hands around her mother's neck. She was used to this demanding, sometimes overwhelming need of her mother's. 'Are the stories true, Mamsa?'

'Not really, pet, they're not really true and yet I suppose they are true in another way. They're true because they say something that's true, something real is going on behind the story.'

Patty said nothing. She patted her mother gently on the back of the neck and then began to draw back from her. 'Mamsa, sometimes I get these headaches . . .' she began.

The birds that flitted among the reeds out on the lake often attracted Patty's attention. They were small, some of them had little black heads, like sparrows, and a white collar; others were a dull brown with small black stripes. They were always busy, flying hurriedly about the reeds and across the water, then off over the surfaces of the bog and about the bushes, and back again, the low tseek, tseek, tseek of their call a quick scratch on the glass surface of the day, and sometimes they made a chinking noise, as if they were rattling keys somewhere down in their throats. Their busyness filled the day with life and emphasised the stillness that Patty loved to feel about her. Sometimes, too, a water hen would skate out onto the lake from somewhere under the banks and impatiently fuss about before returning to its secret stores and nests.

One day she sat, grown older, her eyes watching the lapping of the water at the very edge of the lake, her right hand idly sifting sand back into the water. The Captain, she knew, was away at the harbour and would not be back until it was time for prayers. Her mother was, as usual, sitting in the parlour, curtains drawn against the light of the afternoon; Patty knew she often cried to herself in there, a dry, gasping way of crying, a sobbing that was without tears. The girl did not understand why Nora sat like that, so often, alone, in the dark, sobbing. It was such a lovely day, too, warm and still, the purple flowers of the rhododendron bushes wide open to the sun.

Suddenly Patty looked up, aware of an intense silence that seemed to have swollen out of the day about her. She noticed that the small birds were not visible anywhere; there were no bird sounds to be heard. She glanced about her with a small uneasiness. The world was empty, the brown heathlands stretching emptily away. Only the softly lapping waters of the lake were there to re-assure her. She held the little fistful of sand without moving.

Then she heard it, a sound that seemed to come from behind the invisible curtains of the air, to be low in the texture of the hills on the other side of the lake, to be rising out of the flanks of the mountain into the silence of the day. It was a long, long calling sound, as of an animal far away in the deep distance. It was so low, so distant, Patty was not even sure if she was hearing it, if it was not simply the echo of the day's stillness sounding in the blood of her brain. But it frightened her, held for so long, fading slowly back into the hills. She stood up, watching across the water of the lake. She did not hear it again. Silence only.

She had to cry out as a stab of pain struck her in the right hand. She opened her hand wide and the sand dripped out and made small sluicing sounds in the water. She held up her hand before her face to look at it; her fingers had gone rigid, all except her thumb, she could not move them, they were stretched, misshapen, white, the knuckles standing out hard under the flesh. She cried with the pain of it and began to run back down the cart track toward her home. As she ran the pain began to ease and her stiffened fingers relaxed.

She told the Captain that evening, told him about the long cry she had heard the mountain give, about the pain that had stiffened her fingers into immobility. He held her hand and looked at it; he saw nothing. Nothing but the small, delicate and beautiful hand of a young, young girl.

'Must have been a cramp from being in the cold water of the lake,' he reassured her. 'Just a cramp, that's all.'

'And the headaches I get, Dodgie?'

'I'll get Doctor Weir to come and see about the headaches, I promise. Maybe you're out in the sun too much.'

'And was the sound I heard a real one?'

'I don't know, pet, maybe it was just Johnnie Trawlie's hound you heard, moaning about his old age. Or maybe you just imagined it. Could you have imagined it?'

'You mean it wasn't real, Dodgie, like the stories?'

'It might have been there all right, pet, but there would be some good explanation for it, you can be sure. Some good explanation.'

The Captain watched over the edge of the pier down into the water. The ocean was clear and blue and he could see on the sandy bottom the corpse of a dogfish swaying languidly with the swell of the tide. An ugly fish, he thought, fat-fleshed, sick-coloured grey, trying to be a killer shark in a world far too great for him. Putting on airs and graces, a bully among sprat. And now look at him, mocked in death by the very medium in which he lived and hunted. And what, he wondered, does the ocean do with its endless stream of corpses? Digest them back into itself as the earth does hers? To spew them out again in a billion billion eggs for rehatching, for resurrection, back to the hunt, the slaughter, feeding, death? For some reason, then, the image of his daughter, Patty, floated before his mind, Patty, small and innocent, yet so alone in the world. If only, he thought, if only Nora were stronger, we might – a son, now, a son, wouldn't that be something? Something for them all, for him, for Nora, for Patty.

The Captain watched the great black body of a basking shark being winched slowly up the slipway. Machines failed and caught, chugging laboriously, coughing smoke into the air above the pier. The huge steel ropes strained and twanged against the concrete. A sunfish, as big as a half-decker, ugly and sad and broken by the harpoons of men.

'A fine beast, that,' said one of the men waiting beside the Captain.

The men were dressed in their oldest clothes, heavy rubber aprons wrapping them round, waders making their whole bodies sweat. Soon they would be walking on the exposed flesh of the Leviathan, slithering on its blood and innards, hacking and hooking its flesh and parts into different areas of the sheds.

'A giant, Eamonn, surely,' the Captain replied. 'Will keep us in wages a wee while longer. You'd wonder about the sea, how it throws up such monsters,' he added.

'A harmless monster, then,' Eamonn said. 'Wouldn't harm a shrimp, they say, only to suck the plankton in through its mouth.'

'It has a mouth on it as big as Father Crowe's,' the Captain commented, 'only Father Crowe's blows out more fluid than the shark's. But look at the size of the brute. Reminds me of the German ship that anchored right in that spot during the war, the whole navy of them that came stomping up the road there till me and Tony drove them off again.'

'The German buckos were a sight more dangerous than that shark, Captin,' Eamonn said diplomatically. He paused. 'And what do you think about this other monster, the bogman? I see that Vinnie Scollon has been about, askin' who's lost sheep and such up on the mounting. You'd swear he was beginnin' to believe in the bogman himself.'

'The bogman, Eamonn?'

'The abominable bogman, that's what they do be sayin'. But nobody has seen him, or it, or whatevers.'

'All nonsense, nonsense, all the creation of an overripe imagination. That's all.'

'I don't know, all the same; there's many's the man has lost sheep up there on the back slopes, never been found, and here and there there's those that has seen bits and pieces of sheep left behind, ripped to pieces, maybe a skull left, or a little heap of bones.'

'Crows, Eamonn, the hooded crow. He's a devil, the hooded crow. Or maybe a plague of black-backed gulls. And there were golden eagles up on those slopes known to carry away a full-grown sheep betimes.'

'Ay, but only eat the flesh, only the flesh. An' leave the bones and wool behind them, they did. Not like now. Whatever's happenin' up there, the entire sheep has disappeared, skull and bones and wool and all, everythin'.'

The Captain looked at him. Eamonn was a middle-aged, serious man, his face brown as tree bark from the winds. He stood, resting his body on the great iron hook he'd use to swing portions of the shark's quivering flesh into the back of the lorry. Soon the truck would leave, heading away across the island towards the factory, leaving on the air a thick, nauseating stench of shark meat.

'Seems this thing, if it's up there, has made buck-leps down out of the hills, as close as Casimir Conlon's shed and that's not too far from you, Captin. It's supposed to have carried off some of Casimir's slaughtered sheep.'

'Yes, I've heard that, Eamonn. But he seems to think it was some of the local young lads, out for fun and maybe a bit of a skite.'

'There's people worried, Captin, I can tell you that, worried. Whatever it is, there's havoc been wreaked up in them hills, bird or beast or bogman, an' it won't stay forever in the hills, but'll come down, prowlin'; an' soon, wait and see if I'm wrong, Captin, soon the men will stop pasturin' up there forever, up on them slopes.'

The grinding and whining of the machinery had stopped. The mighty carcass lay high on the pier, alongside the waiting sheds. Men with long reaping hooks had begun hacking at the fins and tail; others drew their blades along the black glistening skin, gouging furrows into the thick flesh. Soon the skin would settle into a dulled grey, the white rippling flesh would fall into a sour-cream yellow, the stench would fill the air about the pier and over-whelm the senses of the men. The concrete tanks would fill with liver oil. The furnace would cheer on the bones and offal.

Together the two men walked slowly towards the carcass. The

men already working were shouting and calling, urgent, intent.

'Seems like he do be right, though,' Eamonn said. 'Father Crowe, I mean. Even in the mist of life we are in death. The mist of life, Captin, when we can see hardly our own hand's length in front of our own faces. True words, true for him, I'd say.'

'Midst,' proferred the Captain, halfheartedly. 'In the *midst* of life.'

'Ay, the mist,' Eamonn said. 'The mist of life. Life's a queskin, after all, a hard, hard queskin. With no answer, Captin, with no answer.'

Finding nothing more to say to Eamonn's words, the Captain turned with a grimace of disgust towards his task.

5

S he could have been a child again, trudging westwards through the morning, fragile as porcelain, the clothes motley, the wellingtons clumsy. Out of her pain and weariness she yet found strength to urge herself forward. Walking from one telephone pole at the side of the road to the next; resting a while; then moving on to the next pole, resting again. Slowly, so slowly. And yet she walked with confidence, knowing her destination, sure of it, knowing she would find the courage, the grace necessary to see it through. Wasn't she Mary now, hurrying with her news to Elizabeth? A long journey over hill country, her being big with the future. She could even exult at the thought, those short moments she rested, panting, beside a pole.

Day was coming up all about her, silver, cold and taxing. But she, in her hurry, was already hot. The clothes had dried against her flesh, the red plastic coat was rolled up and held under her arm. When a morning dawned as bright as this one, she knew it would cloud over quickly, there would be rain. Even here, in this dry land. Palestine, wasn't it? The hill country. She clutched her stomach with a sense of sudden pain. He couldn't have kicked already. Or could he? How long ago? Since the . . . since . . . since what?

She stopped. She looked away over the dull, tarred road before her. This was not Palestine. She was being foolish. There was nothing in her stomach. Hunger, perhaps, that was all. She hadn't eaten. Except for a few late blackberries that gleamed like small black stars in the green sky of the hedge. Nothing but blackberries, since that flaccid, insipid stuff last evening. Poached egg. More tepid water than egg. But it would be enough to keep her going. For today. Her hunger now wasn't that kind of hunger. Not now. Not ever again.

She shivered. And walked on. Steadying herself. She must remain calm. And she must keep her mind pure. Alert. And on target. To find the mulberry tree, the mulberry tree, the mulberry tree, and stand under it, looking up at its fruits of snow. She would wait, unafraid of wild animals, of lions or tigers or bears, unafraid even of wolves, she would wait, and he would come, she would fling her arms about him, forgive him all his unfaithfulness, for he was young, and good-willed, perhaps he had been tempted, and was weak. She loved him still, loved him even more because of his frailty, his small human life that tried only to carry its own weight safely through the world. *Joshua? Thisbe?* Josh. That was it, Josh. She would prevent his death. There would be no blood to stain the snowfruit red. And then they could lie down together, here and now and side by side, in the same tomb.

There came to her out of her dreams the sound of an engine in the distance. She looked about, anxiously, almost panicking. There were bushes to her left. She pushed her way in among them. They tore at her clothes like living things. At her flesh. She thought how the lion had destroyed poor Thisbe's life. She looked out through the bushes at the morning. A bus was coming towards her, its sound harsh on the morning air. The sun was moving higher into the sky. The bus, painted red and white, was full of people, all of them on the watch for her, to trap her, to bring her back to pain and humiliation. They would not see her.

She pushed herself further back into the cave of the bushes.

When her father got the sudden idea to become a gardener, her mother had muttered something about layabouts, and all the acres begging for real things, for spuds and cabbages and carrots and peas, but he had sent for books and catalogues and had decided on growing row upon row of giant sunflowers. What a wonderful idea that had been! Row upon row of giant sunflowers. Taller than she was, they had stooped their wondrous faces down towards hers and she had laughed up at them, into their knowing eyes. But now she couldn't remember if the garden had ever been created, if she had really walked in it, if she had ever lived under the golden light of sunflowers.

The bus passed, she could see the tense, strained faces; they did not see her; they were intent on looking in the wrong direction. Looking forward, or looking into their own lives with dulled, unseeing eyes. The road shuddering as the bus went by, then it was gone. She waited for silence to return. Then she stepped back out onto the road.

From pole to pole. Resting each time perhaps a moment longer than before. Too tired then to hide from car or bus. Thirsty, too. The sun blazing down. All that sand. Everywhere. And lizards slithering rapid as thoughts across her flesh. Barrenness all around. The beginnings of a harsh buzzing somewhere above her head. And the warm winds blowing only sand into her face. She closed her eyes. Tight. If even she could cry. Wash away the sand and grit from her eyes. From her soul. But she could not cry. She was too dry. Too empty.

She shook her head quickly and opened her eyes. She sat to rest on a stone by the side of the road. Behind her – across the road and away over the valleys – the great pyramidal shape of a mountain rose like a blessing over the land. Croagh Patrick. Heath and moor and silence. Not a breath of wind, not a sound from bird or beast or man. This could be the very beginning of the world, she thought, or the very end. All of creation benevolent, as if the great disease of death had never taken root in the flesh of humankind. Silence. Distance. Calm. For a long moment, a long, delightful moment, she knew something approaching peace. And then she heard the low drone of an engine.

There was something coming towards her along the road. She

closed her eyes. She did not have time or energy to hide. She could hear the sounds of the vehicle as it slowed and drew in to the side of the road not far from her. Her whole body sagged. She knew what the phrase meant, *when the spirit droops*. She knew that soon she would hear a door open. Footsteps. Heavy. They would approach her where she sat. Her whole body swayed in anticipation of her capture. She recoiled. She would hide within herself, within her own spirit where she might find refuge from the world. She drew away from the road, from the day, from time. Drew deeper into the heaviness of herself. Down into the easing darkness of a cave underground. Down. Deeper. Before the hand could touch her.

6

L ight fell from the window onto the rough ground of the yard. The night was still, chill and dark. Inside the room Patty had said her prayers, kneeling as she always did by the side of her bed:

0 angel of God, my guardian dear,
to whom God's love commits me here,
ever this night be at my side
to light and guard, to rule and guide.

The Captain had not come home. Patty lay quietly, a sadness settling about her at his absence. He would come in very late tonight, and very drunk. Or he might not come home at all and then he could be gone for days, leaving Nora spent, but relieved. In Patty the tension was always worst when he did not appear, not knowing when he would come home, not knowing what condition he would be in when he did return. Now the words kept repeating themselves, over and over and over in her mind: *to light and guard, to rule and guide; to light and guard to rule and guide; tolightandguard, toruleandguide.* Nora was still down in the parlour; she would stay there, in the darkness, until she was sure the Captain was not coming home, then she would go wearily to bed.

Patty reached out and turned off the light. The deep darkness settled at once, though inside her eyes the light still sparkled and danced. She curled down into the bed. For a while she could not even begin to try and sleep, listening intently for the Captain's footsteps on the road outside, or the swinging aggression of a song. Then she would hear the squealing of the gate being opened and its bolt clanging shut. At that point, she knew, the Captain would try to go quietly, steadying himself, preparing to face the depression, the silence, the distant reproach of Nora waiting for him in the darkness. Tonight, however, Patty heard none of these sounds. She began to drift away toward sleep.

A faint rustling noise from the pine grove brought her fully awake. The silence in the room was a humming silence. She opened her eyes to an almost total darkness. She sat up in bed, listening.

For some time she heard nothing. Then there came that rustling noise again, as if someone were moving stealthily through the grove. She wondered if it could be the Captain, trying to creep back into the house unnoticed. That would be unlike him. She slipped out of bed and drew the curtains back ever so slightly.

There was a faint suggestion of light outside from a moon she could not see. The vague shapes of the trees were discernible against the darkness. She thought she noticed some movement amongst the escallonia bushes inside the boundary wall of the grove. She could not be sure. All was silent. She stood for a while, watching. Soon, however, she realised that she was cold. She let the curtains fall together again and moved quickly back towards the bed. The suddenness of the pain in the back of her neck made her cry out, a quick jab of pain that was as vicious as the cramp that had caught her by the lake. She fell forward onto the bed and lay on it, sobbing quietly under the assault. It seemed to shift then, quickly, down into the shoulder blades. She stretched her upper back, trying to find ease. The pain vanished as quickly as it had come, leaving her shaking and crying quietly into her hands. She climbed awkwardly and carefully back into bed.

After a long time she slept, a shifting, restless sleep. Far within that sleep she stepped out onto a road paved with nails and glass and her feet were naked and someone, perhaps the Captain, perhaps Nora, someone frantic and insistent called her, waved and beckoned and urged her forward. She moved onto the glass and nails and they pierced the soles of her feet. And still the calling persisted, the hand waving, the blank face pleading.

She woke suddenly. There was a pain knifing through her head. She opened her eyes on a darkness that seemed to leave flashes of vermilion light in it as the pain stabbed her. She breathed hard, trying to stay calm. Trying not to call out. She sat up in bed again and held her head in her hands; she closed her eyes against her suffering. The pain eased, settling into a dull throbbing ache. She was certain she heard the same shuffling sound through the pine needles on the floor of the pine grove. She wondered if the Captain were home, if she could go to him.

When she heard a faint moaning sound from beyond her window her whole body stiffened with fear and her eyes opened wide again onto the darkness. It was an animal noise, she thought, a moan of an animal in pain. The moaning stopped. She listened. Then there came the sounds of quickly intaken breaths, a sigh, a sob, almost human. Distant sounds, and close, real sounds, yet imagined, too. Someone must be hurt and unable to call out, she decided. The Captain? Some traveller? Silence again. And all the time there was that dull pain throbbing in her head.

Although she was frightened she got out of bed and approached the curtains cautiously. She could see nothing through the darkness. There was silence, apart from a gentle night breeze moving softly through the tips of the trees. She waited. Gradually the pain eased away from her, like a fog rising before the dawn. A minute. Two. Five. She heard nothing. She began to feel sleepy again. Softly she let the curtains drop. She got back into bed. She slept.

The Captain laughed at her when she told him.

'Was it you, Dodgie, creeping home?'

'Me? When did you ever know me to creep home?'

'What was it then, Dodgie, maybe somebody was hurt?'

'A cat, maybe, crying for a mate,' he said.

She knew it was not a cat.

'An owl, maybe, sometimes owls come through those trees at night. Calling. Making strange sounds.'

He went with her, in through the small wooden gate, in under the wonderful trees, the fragrance of the resin rich in the noonday warmth. All was still, the gloomy peace was undisturbed. They searched about near the bushes opposite Patty's window but there was nothing, nothing but the disturbance of leaves and pine needles made by their own passing. Gently he ruffled her hair.

'The world is a funny place,' he told her. 'There are animals, birds, all sorts of things that live and hunt only by night. They hunt and they kill. Their prey might cry out, Patty, or be exhausted and panting from the chase. On a quiet night you could hear nothing at all and yet the hunting and killing would be going on. Something like that you heard, something as simple as that. I'll get Doctor Weir to see about those headaches you're getting.'

Unquieted, she left the grove, closing the little wooden gate, and walked slowly away, wondering. She knew her mother sometimes walked in there, inhaling the wooden gloom, relishing the dimness of the light, the scent of decay that rose from the damp earth.

'Oh, darling, no,' she said. 'I'd never go out there in the dark of night. Never.'

Nora was raking the ashes from the cooker in the kitchen. It was hot and stuffy in there and Patty watched her mother's back stooped over the stove. Then she got down on her hands and knees on the floor, sighing, working. Ashes, the cleaning, the daily round; wood, into flames, into ash, into soil, into wood, into . . .

'Why are you always sad, Mamsa?'

Nora stood up slowly and looked at her. She waited a moment. Then she wiped her hands in her apron. 'It's something in my head,' she said quietly. 'Something that has no real reason to it. There are things in our lives that we cannot put a real name to, darling, but that does not mean they're not real. What I suffer from has a kind of a name. It's depression. And I can't get rid of it. It's like – clouds.

Dark clouds that you can feel pressing you down into the ground. Dodgie calls it nerves. Doctor Weir gives me tablets but they only make me heavier, wanting to sleep all the time. And I don't want to go to hospital, I'd be in there for weeks, months maybe. And even then they wouldn't be able to get rid of it.'

She reached out and drew her daughter close to her. 'You won't let them bring me off to the home, sure you won't, precious? Promise me that. Promise me!' She drew Patty's head against her breasts and gazed over her towards the window and the grove beyond. 'Any bit of happiness I have is here with you and Dodgie, and this house, and my love for you. They mustn't take that away from me. It's all I have. It's everything. You won't let them, precious, sure you won't?'

Patty was crying quietly against her mother's breasts. 'I promise, Mamsa, I promise,' she whispered.

That night Patty did not sleep. It was warm and a soft breeze moved through the darkness. There were stars. She heard her mother go down the hallway to her room. She heard the door open and close behind her. Patty lay on, imagining the sobs of her mother in that room, her helplessness, the weight of sadness that lay upon her. Soon she heard the Captain go to the front door and lock it, she heard him move quietly to the back door; she heard the dull iron thuds of the bolts. She heard him climb the stairs to the small room in the attic. Nora and the Captain didn't sleep together any more.

There was a thin ribbon of wheaten light falling from the split in the curtains across Patty's bed and touching the wall opposite. She gazed at it, idly. She wondered if she would ever sleep again. For some reason then she turned and glanced toward the curtains. There was something at the window, watching her. She was certain she glimpsed the outline of a head, two eyes staring in at her out of the darkness, big eyes, grey, or black, she remembered later, but she thought there was a touch of light green colour from them, too. For a second she stared back at those eyes, then she screamed and screamed, her hands raised to her head, her eyes closed. She screamed, she thought, for hours, before the door burst open and it was Nora who came running in and switched on the light. Patty was sitting up in bed, pointing towards the window.

'Hush, hush, hush!' Nora whispered and took her in her arms.

The Captain came in, in his dressing gown. Patty was sobbing hysterically, her face buried in her mother's bosom.

'She said she saw a face at the window, looking in at her,' Nora told him quietly.

The Captain whipped aside the curtains. There was nothing there, nothing visible except the reflected image of the brightly lit room. He hurried outside; they heard him unbolt the back door, they heard him moving round on the gravel of the yard outside the window. Then he came in, bolting the door behind him.

'Must have been a nightmare, sausage-face,' he said when he came back into the room.

Patty looked up at him. Nora was soothing her hair, whispering softly to her. Her face was pale, wet with tears.

'You imagined it, or you dreamed it, that's all,' he went on. 'There's nobody out there. The gate is closed, the grove gate is closed. The window is high. Someone would have had to climb up on something to look in. There's no marks. There's nothing out there.'

Patty stared at him, still trembling. She said nothing. Nora settled her back down in the bed.

'Sometimes,' Patty whispered, 'things don't have names, but that doesn't mean that they're not real.'

'I'll sleep with you tonight, pet,' Nora said. 'Together we'll sleep. We'll be safe together, we'll be safe.'

Patty closed her eyes. Her body still quivered under the shock, her face looked small and wan and helpless against the pillow.

The Captain shook his head, slowly. He felt hurt by life, its cruelty to those who are most gentle, its roughness towards those most worthy of care. He felt helpless before these two suffering beings in his care, the two people he loved most on the earth.

It was early evening. The Captain stood at the crossroads, watching out for the bus. Izabel had sent one of her cryptic telegrams from

Dublin: 'CONSIGNED EVENING BUS STOP STOP STOP'. He had not been able to figure it out. He assumed, after consulting Nora and Patty, that one of her famous Christmas packages was about to materialise during the summer months and that they were to stop the evening bus and collect it. Consigned. As the day leaked away towards evening, a certain tremor of excitement could be felt throughout the house.

The bus appeared over the hump of a hill about two miles away. It would dip in through the valley and disappear. Then it would be heard again, urging itself up the hill towards the crossroads, its groans suggesting enormous stress. When it appeared it would be less than a quarter of a mile away, its green bulk telling of rhythms of emigration and return, of fair days and pilgrimages, of old men departing sober and returning intoxicated by what they had found in the town, many miles away.

The Captain stuck out his left hand. The bus drew in toward him. He nodded encouragement to Peter Lyons, the driver, who was sitting hot and bothered in his cabin. Peter grinned at the Captain and the latter drew himself up along the frail string of his dignity. Izabel was handed down from the bus.

'Holy Mother of my Divine Jesus!' the Captain muttered.

Izabel stood on the damp, grassy margin of the road, distressed that her feet should be so close to mud. The conductor, Willie Quinn, in shirt sleeves, grinning too, skipped out of the bus and disappeared behind it. He began climbing up the ladder at the back, to the rack on the roof. After some moments, while Izabel and the Captain stared at each other across enormous distances, he came round the back of the bus again, touched his forehead in salute to Izabel, winked at the Captain and murmured, 'Captain! Lovely evening, praise God!' then hopped cheerily back onto the bus.

'Holy Mother of my Divine Christ preserve us!'

Brother and sister held their distance from one another in utter silence. It was a duel, venomous as those at dawn, under trees, with pistols, once held in secret at the back edges of the world. The eyes sending messages of distrust, antagonism, even hatred; the bodies straining backward from one another without moving, straining; the silence between them deadly as blades.

'It's me, Cyril. It's Izabel.'

'I didn't think it was the Virgin Mary!'

She smiled, a hard smile, forced up from the depths of her meagre strength. She was smaller than ever, shrunken, lost in a beige suit that came far below her knees, a black, furred square hat sitting rakishly on her head. She was heavily made up with powder and a lipstick far too bright for her pale face.

She used her best weapon. She turned her head towards her two suitcases and nodded at them. 'Would you be very kind and bring them inside for me, Cyril?'

'Oh! you are stopping the night, then, Izabel, are you?'

She smiled again. 'I thought I might stop a while and look after my little Izabel.'

The Captain winced. 'Nora and I are quite capable of looking after Patty, thank you. But you're welcome to stay the night, now you've come this far.'

She paused. She had a riposte. She held it back.

Once again the silence grew between them like a balloon. Then she yielded to him, she seemed to droop before him, grow feeble and wizened. The Captain noticed how the creams and powder covering her face seemed to hang here and there in visible ridges. The black fur hat was pressed down on her grey and thinning hair. For a moment, as the Captain sensed on the air her bitterness against life, he knew he should be feeling sorry for her, aged and decrepit years before her time. He was stout, red-faced, a man of the world, a man with influence, riding high on thermals of air about his own place, his home.

He said nothing but moved slowly toward her suitcases. She began to hum tunelessly to herself and the sound grated at once through the Captain's bones.

She walked ahead of him toward the house. 'How is Noreen?' she asked over her shoulder.

He did not allow this to upset him. He picked up the suitcases. They were heavy. 'Have you been stealing the paving stones from the streets of Dublin, Izabel?'

Her back, as she moved ahead of him, was bent. She reminded him suddenly of a daddy-long-legs, a harvester, at the end of the season, desperately gripping to some rough wall surface, and trembling away its last pathetic moments. Could he be kind to her? Could he tolerate her, even for a while?

She offered no explanation. They settled her into the room upstairs. The Captain shifted himself, lumberingly, complaining, back into Nora's room. He moaned and grumbled. She stood on the landing outside the room, torturing a white lace handkerchief between her hands. And humming.

'Will you be staying long?' he asked her, exasperated.

'It depends, Cyril dear,' she said, smiling quietly.

When he was about done she opened one of her suitcases and handed him a can of DDT.

'Sprinkle that around the floorboards for me, Cyril, please,' she asked him, 'and on the top of the stair. I know what this house is like for cockroaches.'

In her kitchen Nora groaned and sank further into the soft mud of her life. Only Patty remained quiet before the presence, as if she knew something. She was thirteen now, pretty, petite, her breasts already beginning to shape her dress, her eyes grown still and deep, reflective, like corrie water.

The next day Nora sent her daughter to Conlon's for lamb chops. 'Good thick lamb chops, pet.'

'But Izabel won't eat meat, Mamsa, especially not Conlon's mutton.'

Nora only smiled at her and said nothing.

Casimir was sitting on a low stool outside his premises, his off-white apron screwed up about him. He was reading the *Independent*, Rip Kirby, Curly Wee and Gussie Goose. The easy hooks of the rhymes. The engaging pictures. Fur and Feather Land.

'And how is my own little Patty O'Higgins today?'

'Well, Mr Conlon, very well, thank you.'

Casimir watched her cross the trodden ground. He noticed the young breasts, the shape of her ankles. He pursed his lips tight and folded up his newspaper.

'Aunt Izabel has landed, Mr Conlon,' she volunteered, to change the direction of his thoughts. 'And we'd like some of your best lamb chops, please.'

'Your Aunt Izabel, is it now?' Casimir was interested. He went into the dimness of his shop.

Patty looked towards the cowpat brown door. 'How is Pee-Wee, Mr Conlon?'

'Fine as any galloping horse, the old bag,' he whispered at her, touching his nose with the tip of one finger. 'She'll live for ever, the old cow.'

'Would she be a horse or a cow, Mr Conlon, now? You'd better decide.'

There came the inevitable, unintelligible shriek from the cavern beyond. Casimir gazed, a saint, towards the ceiling.

'It's Patty O'Higgins, come for chops,' he roared.

There was silence from the room beyant.

'She'll be asking me all now,' Casimir went on quietly, as his great cleaver struck the meat. 'So. Your Aunt Izabel. How long might she be staying, now?'

'I really don't know, Mr Conlon.'

'Is there an anniversary, or a wedding, or ay something?'

'Nothing like that, Mr Conlon. Only a visit.'

Casimir wiped his hands along his apron. He began wrapping up the chops in brown paper. 'She's very well off, I hear tell, your Izabel?'

'Very well off, Mr Conlon. A house in Dublin crammed full with gold.'

He glanced at her. 'Dublin. Yes.' He sounded doubtful. 'Still, I suppose a body'd get used to the big city after a year or two, wouldn't you think, Patty?'

'After chasing sheep over the mountainsides it might take a dozen or so years, Mr Conlon.'

As she left the shop she knew Casimir was already on his way down the corridor towards the cowpat brown door.

They sat at table. Patty was animated. Izabel sat back a little, her handkerchief in her hand, prepared. The Captain sat at the head of the table. Waiting.

Izabel sniffed. 'Will you tell Noreen I'll only have a small piece of toast, Izabel dear,' she said.

'Oh now, Izabel,' the Captain intervened. 'We have the loveliest slices of the arse-end of a dead sheep for ourselves today. Casimir Conlon's very best. Cut and carved with his own fair hands. You must taste. You must keep your strength up while you're with us, you know.'

Izabel glanced toward Patty. She sniffed again. 'You know I never eat meat, Cyril. And your mountain sheep would be far too tough for me.'

Nora came from the kitchen and put a bowl of potatoes in the centre of the table. They steamed beautifully, their jackets hanging loose to reveal the fine white flesh. Nora came again and placed a plate before the Captain, and one before Izabel. There was a big chop on each plate, a large portion of yellow-white fat bubbling along the edge of each chop. With cabbage . . .

Izabel brought her handkerchief to her nose. She paused. She turned to Patty. 'Izabel dear, perhaps you'll bring me just one slice of buttered toast up to the room after you've had your dinner?'

Patty nodded, crestfallen.

Izabel rose delicately, stepped back and pushed her chair in under the table. 'Cyril will add my piece of meat to his own, I'm sure.' She spoke quietly, moving slowly out of the room. She did not bang the door.

The Captain grinned. They could hear her going up the stairs to her room. The Captain reached across the table for Izabel's plate.

'It's not fair, Dodgie,' Patty said, quietly.

'Humph! Landing in on top of us without a word of warning. Without as much as a by-your-leave. And one hand as long as the next and her as well off as Rockefeller!'

'It's not fair, that's all, it's just not fair.'

He speared the extra chop with his fork and landed it, like a captured fish, on his own plate.

Izabel braved the table again at supper time. They sat in their places, a mist of tension and silence enveloping them. Izabel tinkered with a slice of home-made bread and blackberry jam. She did not raise her eyes from her plate. She wiped the lip of her teacup with her handkerchief; then, cautiously, she took a tiny sip.

Nora was exasperated. 'I did wash the cup, you know, Izabel!'

'I have no doubt you did, Noreen. No doubt at all.'

More exasperated than ever, Nora struck again. 'I believe Casimir Conlon is throwing eyes at you, Izabel. Now, wouldn't you be doing very well there?'

There was a long pause. The air froze into glass.

'A man is a beast and a craven thing,' Izabel replied, speaking scarcely above a whisper.

'Casimir has a wonderful aftershave lotion,' the Captain joined in. 'A mixture of fresh meat scented with offal.'

Izabel dropped her slice of bread onto the plate. She opened her mouth to speak.

'You're horrible!' It was Patty who slammed her hands down on the table. She was near to tears. 'You're mean, both of you, mean. I only said that Casimir was asking about Aunt Izabel. That's all. There was nothing else. Nothing!'

'Shush, child, shush, it doesn't matter.' Izabel leant towards her, smiling. Then she repeated, quietly. 'It really does not matter.'

Izabel turned to the abashed couple and spoke firmly. 'I came to this house to find out about all these aches and pains that Izabel suffers from. She has written to me about them. I am anxious to find out if I can help.'

Nora glanced towards her daughter and her face was ashen with despair. 'Doctor Weir says it's a touch of arthritis she has.' Nora spoke in a voice that was heavy and unsure, allowing the whole weight of grief and uncertainty into her words.

'I know all about your Doctor Weir, Noreen. He's a fool. The child is scarcely thirteen. She cannot have arthritis. And it has not been in our family.'

Patty sat quietly, her head lowered.

'I'm sorry, Izabel,' the Captain murmured. 'I am sorry. But we have been worried about her. The doctor has been many times. He says she may also have a bit of rheumatism. Between the two it causes pains in her joints and muscles and gives her headaches. He says we must build her up. Make her strong. Give her plenty of vitamin c. Give her sunshine. Iron. And he has given her something to ease the pains.'

'Thank you, Cyril, thank you.' Izabel was at ease now, and in command. She sat up straight and seemed to have grown in stature. Her voice was firm. Her face, cleared of make-up, although it was deeply lined and very pale, seemed to take on a memory of her former beauty. 'I have seen more suffering in my time,' she offered, 'than was good for any human being to see. I have known children to suffer from various forms of rheumatoid-arthritis. And one of the things you must *not* do is keep her out in the sun. You must guard her eyes, you know. Her eyes.'

'Eyes?' Nora queried.

'Yes, Nora, her eyes. And you must stop filling her brain with all these silly stories. She has a vivid imagination, you know, your daughter has. You must not fill her mind with nonsense.'

'Nonsense?' Nora queried.

'Nora, you are positively an echo in the room. Nonsense, yes, that's what I say. Tales of wolves and witches and spells. You have her hearing noises and seeing devils and keeping herself awake all night. No wonder the child has headaches.'

The Captain glanced at his daughter. She was crying soundlessly and Izabel's right hand lay gently on her shoulder.

'I know a very good doctor,' Izabel continued. 'A woman doctor. In Dublin. I propose to bring Izabel with me and get her a thorough examination. A second opinion can do no harm. I don't trust your Doctor Weir. Your local quack. Iron, indeed. Rhubarb and nettles, no doubt. Quack. And flesh meat. I do believe your rough flesh meat is doing the child no end of harm.'

She pressed Patty's shoulder gently. Nora and the Captain were silent, overwhelmed and confused.

'It's settled then,' she went on. 'Izabel shall come with me on Monday. No doubt you will both be glad to be rid of me. She can skip school for a week. I'm sure what she is learning in the local school she can pick up in a matter of five minutes when she comes home. The holiday will do her good. And I'll telegraph you when you are to collect her from the train.'

The meal proceeded in almost total silence. Nora felt, however, as if a burden had been lifted from her shoulders and she smiled across the table at Patty.

Izabel began to eat with some gusto. 'I will have another cup of that lovely tea, Nora, if I may,' she said then, dropping the words into the new dispensation.

The Captain continued to eat in silence, as if he were now wholly outside the world in which his sister and his daughter were living. Patty smiled quietly to herself, looking at her aunt with admiration.

Doctor Weir knocked cautiously at the back door. Then, without waiting, he opened it. Nora was at the range in the kitchen. She had taken to wearing black as if she had decided she was an old woman. She wore a dark blue apron over her dress, tiny stars of yellow sprinkled across it; she had a large wooden ladle in her hand. The range was dead. Nora gazed at it, abstractedly. She moved the wooden ladle in the air as if stirring something. She did not seem to notice the doctor come in.

He stood a moment, watching her. 'Hello, Nora,' he said.

She was startled. The ladle leapt from her hand. It clattered with a wooden anger against the top of the stove. Nora raised her two hands to her face as if she would scream. When she turned to him her face was white and tense.

'Doctor Weir. You're welcome. I was about to prepare some . . . I was about to . . . Was there something special? Is it just a social call?'

'Are you all right, Nora?'

'Yes, yes, I'm fine.'

She rubbed her hands violently up and down against her apron. She left the ladle on the floor where it had fallen. She began to untie her apron. Her hands were hopeless. She succeeded in making a tighter knot. She smiled, foolishly, and Doctor Weir moved to help her. She was young still, he noticed, still handsome, almost beautiful in a sad, wistful way.

'I had a phone call a few days ago,' he said, carefully. 'From your Izabel, in Dublin. Asking me to call this evening. She said she'd be staying here with you for a few days. Do you know what this is about, Nora?'

She did not answer. She looked into his face a moment, her mouth hanging open, as if she feared what might come out should she speak. Then she brought him through the kitchen, across the hallway and into the sitting room. Patty was at the piano, her fingers listlessly touching notes here and there, the sound like raindrops falling on pools of water, the echo of a non-existent music. Izabel

78

stood, frail and stooped, at a window, gazing out over the garden. She was perfectly still. The Captain got up from his armchair and greeted the doctor heartily. It was dusk in the room, dim and resonant of stillness, heavy with an uneasy peace.

'Hello, Miss O'Higgins.'

The doctor went straight over to Izabel and shook her hand. Together, in the faint light that came from the world outside, they looked small, unarmed warriors together before the power of a mighty universe. Nora vanished, murmuring about a cup of tea. They sat, Patty joining them in a little semi-circle around the empty fireplace. It was a warm evening, slow and still.

There were a few, uneasy conversational pleasantries. And they quickly dribbled down the drain into silence.

The doctor explained that Izabel had phoned him from Dublin and he had said he would not discuss Patty's case over the phone. And that no, he had no objection at all to Izabel's bringing her to Dublin for another examination. He spoke about arthritis, about a lack of iron, about puberty, about rheumatism. Nora brought in a tray with tea and biscuits. They sat on together as a warm darkness settled like a familiar animal about them.

'And what do you think about all this nonsense, Doctor Weir?' Izabel spoke at last. 'About sheep-killing and howls and such like. And it seems to have affected little Izabel's imagination and gives her headaches.'

There was silence for a while. They were sitting like ghosts, uncertain, in a ghostly universe.

'Yes, there's something working havoc up in the hills around here,' the doctor said, quietly. 'I was up there, with Donal Crowe, Father Crowe, and we both sensed something, without seeing anything. Other than a sudden fall of stones, as if something had stirred on the mountainside.'

'And what did you sense, doctor?' The question was put with only a faint trace of sarcasm.

'The abominable bogman!' the Captain interjected, laughing.

'Cyril, do please be quiet. I am speaking to Doctor Weir.'

'Well.' The doctor was hesitant. Patty sat close by Izabel, her body bunched together. She put her hand through Izabel's arm. Izabel took her hand in hers. In the darkness nobody noticed.

'Almost all the men have lost sheep up there, Miss O'Higgins, over a number of years. And several say the population of mountain goats has been decimated in the same period. There was an inexplicable raid on Pat Larry's van, that's closer to home than the mountain slopes, mind you, and closer still, Casimir Conlon claims some of his sheep were stolen out of his slaughterhouse.'

'Thieves and robbers merely,' Izabel snorted.

'Perhaps so, Miss O'Higgins, perhaps so. Perhaps not.' The doctor left his statements hanging on the air, balancing.

'And strange noises?' Izabel probed. 'Little Izabel tells me she has heard them, and others have, too, and it has her worried, you know. Hasn't anyone investigated?'

'Guard Vinnie Scollon has been gathering statements from people. I believe he has scoured the slopes too, without success. It's a wild, barren place up there, Miss O'Higgins, and very extensive, and the winds are rough, the ground treacherous, the cliffs are man killers. There are hidden caves and deep holes in the cliff tops. A man could fall, be lost. The mists, too, come down suddenly on those slopes. You can't spend too long up there, you know, most especially on your own.'

'You are reticent about your own experience, Doctor Weir?'

'Well, Donal Crowe and I sensed rather than found anything, so we are really in no position to comment.'

'But what are we talking about, Doctor Weir?' Izabel persisted. 'Is it human or animal predators, or is it the silly ravings of a lot of island boors?'

'You cannot call chemist and merchant island boors, Miss O'Higgins. Nor myself and Father Crowe, I hope. Both chemist and merchant claim they were driven half out of their wits up there. Yet they saw nothing. They say they heard something all right, a kind of animal howling, they described it.' He hesitated. 'Like a wolf, they said.'

The word came out into the darkness of the room with a cold, chilling fall.

'There have been no wolves in this country for many centuries, Doctor Weir, and I'm pretty sure your chemist and your merchant wouldn't know the sound of a wolf if they heard one. Such foolishness. There must be wild dogs up there, don't you think? Have tracks been found?'

'Not identifiable tracks, Izabel,' the Captain offered. 'Even on the soft peaty soil there have been no tracks found, no tracks that can be clearly posited as being those of any particular creature.'

'Birds, then,' Izabel continued. 'Buzzards, or hawks, or eagles. The golden eagle is known to have carried off animals. But if there is something there, I still believe it likely to be a pack of wild dogs. Your local inter-breeding island dogs. Gone wild and crazy. Rabid even, perhaps. And starved. Such things.'

'Rabid wild dogs, thieves and robbers, buzzards ...' the doctor muttered. 'Whatever it is, it's very, very strange.'

They were silent. The room was almost totally dark now. Patty was gripping Izabel's arm.

'It's not good for little Izabel to be hearing things like that.' Izabel was adamant. 'She's young and impressionable and she's taken to imagining things too, cats and owls and such like become wild ferocious beasts in an atmosphere of doubt and vagueness. And when you're not feeling too strong the mind can very easily be disturbed.'

Nora got up suddenly and switched on the light. They were all startled.

'It's time Patty was in bed now,' Nora said. 'Early Mass tomorrow, then we'll have to get her packed and ready for Dublin. She's going with Izabel on Monday, Doctor. It's important for her to go. And we're all very grateful to Izabel. At least the change will do her good.'

After midnight there was a gentle tapping on Izabel's door. She was sitting, her dressing gown wrapped closely about her, in the bay window, watching out across a landscape beautifully nude under the moonlight. The tapping was so soft she was not sure, at first, that she had heard it. But then it came again. More urgently. Softly she called out, 'Come in, Izabel, come in.'

Patty opened the door as if she were committing a crime. She was in her nightie, her feet were bare, her long black hair loose about her face. At first she did not see her aunt and she stood in the half-open door, lost in a dim and uncertain landscape.

'Over here, pet,' Izabel whispered.

The room glowed with moonlight. In her white nightdress Patty was a small hesitant ghost that closed the door quietly behind her and moved soundlessly across the room towards her aunt. Izabel's dressing gown, big and aristocratic – coffee-coloured flowers on a cream background – looked foolish on this frail old woman.

'Can you not sleep, either, Auntie Izabel?'

A small, boney arm reached towards the girl, drawing her into the alcove. Patty sat on the floor by Izabel's feet. The older woman fondled her hair, gently, gently. Remembering.

'I don't sleep very much, pet. I'm getting old, you know. Quite old. And the less time left you in life the less time you want to sleep. You see? And you? Are you excited about Dublin?'

'Yes, I'm excited. And worried, too. What's happening, Auntie Izabel? Am I going to die?'

'Of course you're not going to die, you silly.'

There was silence. There was a fine fragrance from the older woman, as of lavender and old tea, and a sense of peace settled about the young girl at her feet. The landscape beyond them was rich with a buttermilk white, field and hedgerow and low-pitched cottages visible in the gleam, and further off the silver trackway out over the sea that was the moon's.

'I don't want to die, Aunt Izabel. I'm scared of dying.'

'You must not talk about dying, child. We'll get everything sorted out for you in Dublin, just you wait and see.'

Again there was silence. The older woman fondling the young girl's hair.

'I remember once,' Izabel said in a low, very quiet voice, 'I remember, a long time ago, I was younger then, and there was dying everywhere about me. In the war, you know. When men killed each other without thought. Beasts. There was a man shot down somewhere in the desert and he was brought into the hospital and I nursed him. I nursed him for days and days and days and he got better and he went back flying again. But he said something to me that I have never forgotten. He was a small man, British, very quiet. He was a poet, in his own way. He loved to fly, he used to tell me. He would fly alone as far and as high as he could, after their air battles were over and he had dropped his bombs and was heading home.

'Up he'd fly, up and up and up towards the feet of God. He said he would come out on a world of turquoise blue, clean and blue, so clear and perfect that the blue was almost silver, and the white was almost gold. God's carpet, he called it. God's carpet. The clouds would be far beneath him, soft-looking and fluffy and rolling quietly along, as if you could fall onto them and be buoyed up for ever in their embrace. And he would switch his engine off and let his plane glide silently through this wondrous world, gliding, gliding, gliding. Soon the plane would be diving back towards the clouds and he would scream with pleasure as he came out of the clouds again, suddenly, and there the world would be at his feet, patched and coloured and so beautiful in itself that it would make you want to cry. And only then would he switch the engine on again and hope he would come out of the dive.

'And one day he did not come out of that dive,' Izabel continued. 'One day, they told me months later, he disappeared up above the clouds and they never saw him again, as if he had gone so high the angels had taken pity on him and opened heaven just a tiny crack so he could fly in. And he used to say to me that he knew what dying was, when he was gliding silently through those blue spaces above the clouds, it was like stepping out of the plane, he would say, onto the pathways of air and walking slowly and peacefully into the wonder of all that purity and beauty. Through that little crack in the door of heaven. And that is what he did, I am sure of it, that's the way he died, in harmony with the skies, in harmony with the blue and perfect world he found up there, above all that is beastly and hateful in humankind. Wonderful. Wonderful.'

Patty listened to the soft, almost whispering voice, and was intrigued. 'That's a strange story, Auntie Izabel. You must know an awful lot of wonderful things.'

'I have memories, many, many memories. And my silence. I will always have my silence. But some day, some day, I will speak with you.' And she pressed her hand down gently on the young head beneath her.

There was silence again between them, for a while.

'What do they mean about a creature up in the hills, Aunt Izabel?'

'They're foolish people, child, foolish. They are losing their sheep through stupid husbandry, there are wild dogs, or buzzards up there, or the animals are falling down over the cliffs. But they need a scapegoat, someone they can blame besides themselves because a man does not want to look into his own soul and see his beastliness. Man is a beast, a wretched, scavenging beast, and he does not want to know that that is what he is. They want to pin their own foolishness onto something else. Then they try to give their foolishness and their own fears a name, so they can hate it, and they call it war, they call it the bogman, or beast, or wolf.'

'And the cries I heard, Aunt Izabel, what about them?'

'Hush, child, hush, there are no cries. Or if you do hear something then it is merely a poor night creature, an owl, a fox, who knows?'

'Could it be a wolf, Aunt Izabel?'

'There are no wolves in Ireland, nor have there been for centuries. The poor wolf is a creature of the night and the wild places, and men have never understood him. They hunted him down and destroyed him. There are no more wolves here, child. There are no more wolves.'

'Or ghosts, Auntie Izabel, sometimes it feels like we're being haunted. By ghosts or something.'

The older woman did not laugh. 'In a way we are all haunted, Izabel, all of us. We all have our ghosts. I saw many wolves when I was in Africa. They had plenty to gorge upon, goodness knows! But I grew to admire them. Their togetherness. How they worked always perfectly in harmony, one with the others. A pack. With their own rules and loyalties that no member of the pack would ever break. One night, I remember it very well, I was awake very late, like now, pet, like now, and I walked to the limits of our camp. I did not sleep too well, there was a man I was nursing . . . Anyway, I came upon a pack of wolves, lovely, grey-white creatures, big and silent, watchful, masters of their world. There at the very edge of night, as if they were part of the darkness and part of the dawn at the same time. They saw me too, and I knew no fear. I stood still and I watched them. We watched each other, staring one another down. They did not fear me and I knew I was not their prey. Then, all together, as if there had been a signal, they turned away and began to move back into the darkness, beautiful and silent companions one to another. They moved the way water moves, flowing almost, like water flowing across the earth, fluid, almost shadows. They moved on, away from me, and do you know? They left me feeling desolate, lonely, lost, alone.

'For a long moment I wanted to be one of them. But they left me alone in a world filled with violence and hatred and cruelty. Oh my child, the sufferings I saw. Men tearing each other apart, pointlessly destroying each other, murdering each other, and for what? None of them really knew. Slaughter for the sake of slaughter. Man ought have no fear of the wolf, it is the wolf that fears mankind. We are the creatures that ought to be hunted and destroyed from the face of the earth. We are the curse of God on the world.'

The room filled up with quiet. Slowly the young girl closed her eyes, her head lay back against the woman's knees.

Izabel sat for a long time, listening to the girl's breathing grow quieter and more regular, touching her hair, touching the flesh at the back of her neck. There was a sudden, faint, animal noise from outside. Patty came wide awake again.

'Did you hear that, Auntie Izabel?'

'I heard it, pet, I heard it.'

Izabel was sitting upright in her chair, watching out into the night. The stillness remained undisturbed. Nothing moved. And soon the sound came again, a low moaning call that was almost musical, as a low string on a cello sounds, seductive, resonant, sad.

'That's surely a neighbour's dog,' Izabel whispered, 'hurt, perhaps, perhaps a dog baying at the moon.'

Patty did not answer. Outside, the world lay quiet, a mixture of soft white light and shadows.

'The way water moves,' Patty whispered, 'the way shadows move.'

And then they heard it again, so low and sad they had to strain to hear it. It faded quickly back into silence.

'It's a beautiful sound,' Patty said. 'But it frightens me.'

Izabel said nothing. Her hands lay quietly on the girl's head.

Soon, she thought that Patty was asleep. The child's breathing was regular and a little heavy. Izabel strained to see out into the darkness beyond. All was still. Unmoving. The night world lying in its own stillness, a calm dark pool, corrie water lying under the cold indifference of the sky.

'Look, Auntie Izabel!'

The suddenness of the cry from the girl startled Izabel. Patty was holding both her hands up before the older woman's face. The fingers were stretched and distorted, twisted, old. The knucklebones showed white through the stone-grey skin. Izabel reached out and held them in her wizened, stronger hands and she knew the rigidity and pain that was in the young child's limbs.

'It hurts, Auntie Izabel, it hurts,' the young girl sobbed, turning her face in against the woman's knees.

They fasted, from Saturday midnight until Sunday after Mass. Not a crumb of food to pass the lips, not a drop of moisture to touch the tongue until after Communion breakfast with the Lord. To purify the body and to chasten the mind to welcome the Creator of all purity and truth. To dress in their Sunday best, their best that could never be good enough before the Lord.

They left the house together at nine o'clock. The morning was dull and overcast, the road damp from a pre-dawn rainfall. Patty was brighter in herself and skipped before them on the road.

'You'd think you were only too happy to be getting away from us,' Nora complained sadly. 'Indeed I wouldn't blame you. But today maybe we'll all be happy together.'

Nora was walking ahead with Patty. There was little wind but the air had the chill of moisture within it. Izabel walked smartly beside the Captain, his bulk contrasting strongly with the slight, severely stiffened figure of his sister. He stepped on the outside, anxious for her now, careful of any traffic that might pass them on the road. Once they pulled in and watched as Pat Larry-the-Reek Dineen's great van lumbered by. He blew the horn, three lugubrious, short snorts, then he was past them, leaving a small cloud of exhaust fumes trailing over the road behind him.

At a quarter past nine the big bell in the louvred tower of the church began to peal. Its call, loud and imperious, was muffled by the dullness of the morning. The Captain lifted his cap ostentatiously and greeted everyone by name.

Outside the church, shuffling and murmuring among themselves, hands thrust deep into trouser pockets, the men had already gathered against the wall, protected from the main yard by a squat buttress. Here they would stay, smoking and gossiping until they heard the sound of the Sanctus bell from within. Then they would crowd into the back of the church, kneeling with one knee on handkerchief or cap inside the door, their great red hands urging their chins towards prayer. When the bell rang for Communion they would leave again, filtering quietly out into the day, the same red hands hurriedly sketching the Sign of the Cross over face and chest, they would gather back, like cattle, against the wall and prepare for banter, for assessing the young women as they left the church. A few embarrassed and embarrassing moments offered for their Lord.

Izabel ignored them, passing haughtily by as the Captain hesitated to greet them. He winked at the grinning men, their cigarettes buried in the small brown caves of their palms, and followed his family into the church. Izabel took Patty by the hand and guided her up the centre aisle to take their places in the very first pew. Women to the left, men to the right. Nora genuflected and took her place in the front pew, to the left. Izabel, still holding Patty firmly by the hand, moved at once into the front pew, to the right. The whole congregation seemed to bristle for a moment, eyes met eyes knowingly, mouths moved silently. Patty was stricken, but knelt quietly by her aunt, her eyes lowered, but watchful.

The Captain cramped himself into a bench near the back of the church. Soon he would creep out again to offer his fistful of jokes and jibes to the men outside. He would go to the altar rails for Communion and then take up his place again in the bench before the women turned to come back out. Man to man. Woman to woman. The marble floor of the aisle between them.

Father Crowe was instantly aware of Izabel's stern presence in the first pew. She knelt stiffly upright, her eyes focused on the priest, her lips tightly pursed. He found himself stumbling once or twice over his Latin phrases, conscious of those eyes burning into his back. When he turned to greet his congregation, *Dominus vobiscum*, he felt as if he were addressing this demanding woman only; he felt as if she might rise at any moment during his sermon to challenge him. He kept the sermon short, he kept his eyes turned towards the gallery at the back of the church.

As he handed out the hosts, the acolyte moving swiftly along the altar rails beside him, he dreaded those big clear eyes watching, that mouth poised as if it would snap his fingers off; but when he reached her, her eyes were closed, the tip of her tongue barely protruded from between her clenched lips and he was nervous lest the bread might fall. She stayed at the altar rails a while, her eyes closed, impervious to the shifting of other women waiting to take her place. Father Crowe forgot, for a moment, to move on.

Casimir Conlon's Sunday suit sat on him the way an outboard engine would sit on a bicycle. His tie, a startling pink, was in a permanent knot and hung far below the top, opened button of his shirt. His hair, unruly as a sheepdog's coat, was carefully plastered down with Brylcreem. How the men chortled quietly to themselves when they saw him stride up the centre aisle of the building. Casimir Conlon come to God! How the women smiled and shouldered the easier the burden of their Catholic faith that could hook a great fish like Casimir Conlon and land him out of the ocean of his sinfulness.

He was waiting when the family came out of the church. 'Em, Miss O'Higgins, isn't it?' He came up, smiling wildly, his great hand outstretched towards Izabel.

Izabel paused from her morning's thoughtfulness and proffered a delicate gloved hand in return. He shook it warmly.

'Casimir Conlon's the name. I'm sure you remember. You used to be great with my mother, Mrs Conlon, her they calls Pee-Wee. She told me to pass on her regards. To yourself. You're welcome home, you're very welcome home.'

The Captain eyed Casimir suspiciously. He was waiting for a sharp and incisive insult from his sister to send this forward dog home, tail curled between his legs. But Izabel smiled and kept her hand in his.

'Mr Conlon,' she launched in at once. 'I believe you have some first-hand experience of this wild dog that's up in the hills?'

Casimir, taken aback, his follow-up sentences of reference to the weather hovering already on his lips, was dumbstruck.

'Wild dog, miss?' he managed after a while.

'Yes, yes, yes, this wild dog that seems to be taking your sheep.'

'That's no wild dog, miss, I can tell you that. That's no wild dog. That's something bigger an' more awful nor a wild dog. It come and took my sheep from right in front of my nose and carried them over the bogs and fields without a bother. That's no dog. 'Tis something else is up there, miss, but I'm sure you don't want to know nothing about that.'

'Will you show me, Mr Conlon, will you show me?'

'Show you, Miss O'Higgins? Show you what, ma'am?'

'I want you to bring me up where you last saw this beast, or to wherever you think this beast may be. We must clear up what this is all about.'

Casimir looked helplessly around him, calling soundlessly from the great cavern of his chest.

'Well, man? Are you going to show me, or will I have to ask someone else?'

At that moment, Pat Larry Dineen came out of the church, his prayers said, his troubles placed in the lap of the Lord. He too came to greet the visitor and was asked, in return, the same question.

It was agreed Pat Larry would drive Casimir and Izabel back to the foot of the hills, and up the stone track as far as his lorry could go. Then all three of them would ascend together, as far as Miss O'Higgins could manage without danger from the cliffs and bogholes.

The Captain, hearing of this proposed expedition, insisted he would join them too. 'To offer my protection, seeing as I have this German gun and you never know, a gun might just come in handy up there.'

Less than two hours later, Sunday dinners speedily put away, the four of them began the ascent from Pat Larry's van. Izabel had on a pair of wellingtons belonging to Nora. She was wrapped in a tightly belted overcoat and wore a black fur hat. She had gloves on and strode out fearlessly over the rough ground. Casimir Conlon had changed his Sunday suit and was happy again in his rough serge trousers and old brown cardigan. He too wore a coat, old navy blue degenerated into grey. Pat Larry had put on a pair of wellingtons over his Sunday trousers, and had a big white cardigan thrown over his jacket. The Captain wore a dark green hunting coat over his waders, a hunting cap, dark green too, with earflaps, tied under his chin, and a leather cartridge belt crisscrossing the generosity of his chest. He carried the German rifle, in the proper way, barrel pointing into the earth.

The climb began enthusiastically. The day was still dull and overcast, a slight breeze that had touched them at the church now held from them by the rise of the hill. Casimir went slightly ahead, remembering the path of the climb after his sheep. Behind him Pat Larry was solicitous for the welfare of the woman; the Captain, eager and strong and proud, brought up the rear. They offered only occasional sentences, pointing out how the track petered away into bogland, how the heathers were in full and breathtaking bloom, a pleasing scent moving surreptitiously over their senses. The sky above them was heavy and unwelcoming; there were no sounds other than the breathing of the wind and the distant murmur of the sea.

Soon they passed the old stone hut where Casimir's earlier climb had ended. There were only the fallen stones, nettles growing between them. There was no sign of sheep anywhere, no animals moved on the slopes of the mountain. They carried on, in silence, Izabel labouring among the strong bodies of the men.

After some half an hour Izabel halted, trying to get her breath back. The Captain was instantly at her side, worrying for her, fretting.

'I'm perfectly all right, Cyril, thank you very much, perfectly all right. I've been up mountains before, you know, and over oceans, and across deserts. I am just ever so slightly short of breath at the moment.'

She had turned and was facing back down over the island. Already the world was being laid out, like an exotic carpet. She breathed deeply, inhaling the demanding air, her body straight, the wellingtons too large for her feet. For some moments they all stood quietly, watching over the island, silenced, then they turned back into the climb.

They came over a ridge of the mountain. Down to their right they could see the ocean, grey and dark and heaving under the wind. The breeze caught them as they came over the ridge and they paused again, watching and listening. Ahead there was a small valley, wet and covered in rushes and heathers. Still there was no life to be seen anywhere, no birds, no sheep, no goats. Only the breeze seemed to live here now, moving freely over the mountain meadowlands.

Casimir began to climb again, up the edge of the valley towards the higher slopes. They were labouring now, all of them, the Captain puffing more than the others, Izabel leaning into the air as if her very slightness could be buoyed by it. They climbed for perhaps ten more minutes and topped another ridge high above the valley.

Casimir turned suddenly and caught Izabel's arm. 'Look!' he said, pointing.

Away to the right, down almost precipitous slopes, was a lake, lying under the sky as if it were painted a perfect black. In the shadow of the mountain heights it was still and beautiful, its banks lined with ferns, white rocks rising here and there, a thin stretch of bogland separating it from further cliffs and then the sea.

'Lake Nakeeroga!' Casimir announced proudly.

The others came up on the ridge and they all stood a while, gazing down at the wild beauty of the scene.

As they stood there, gradually they grew aware of a stench that seemed to come with the breeze from a great distance off. Izabel, always fastidious, was the first to notice it. Holding her handkerchief against her face she shook her head and began, very slowly, to climb further up the slope.

'Christ, what a stink!' Pat Larry commented.

'Must be a dead and rotting carcass somewheres about,' said Casimir.

They turned to follow the woman and Casimir bumped into Pat Larry's back as they tried to scramble over a narrow stream. Pat's foot sank into the softness, the water came in over the top of his wellingtons and sloshed around his feet.

'You buggerin' eejit,' he shouted at Casimir, drawing his fist back in readiness.

'Ah, it's your own fuckin' fault. Just move, will you, for Christ's sake!' came the quick hissing answer from the bigger man.

For a moment they stood, glaring at each other, Pat in the water, his fists clenched and prepared, Casimir looming over him from the heather hillock.

'What in God's earth am I doing up here with you pair?' the Captain shouted. 'And I could be at home with a nice glass of whiskey in my fist. Instead of up here in the wet and cold on a wild goose chase with a pair of bickering babies.'

'Oh it's the drink you'd be after sure enough,' retorted Pat Larry. 'You needn't tell us about the drink. You're as wet as this buggerin' stream the fuckin' butcher has shoved me into!'

He was scrambling away towards the other side of the stream, bent double, lifting his heavy wellington out of the slush. It was then that Casimir lunged at him, heaving his body against the lesser man until both of them crashed forward against the wet ditch in a tangle of limbs and coats.

Pat Larry roared with anger and swung out wildly at the butcher. But Casimir was already up again, on his hands and knees, like an animal prepared to rush. The swung fist burst the air near his face and Pat Larry fell on his back in the dampness.

'Come on, then,' Casimir screamed at him, 'come on and show what kind of a man you are.'

He stood over Pat Larry, a tower of bulk and muscle, and as the smaller man tried to rise he dug his knee into his ribs and Pat Larry, with a groan, fell back again on the ground.

'Get up, you fuckin' greengrocer. Get up and face your punishment. Jesus but I'll lave the print of my fist on your guts for ever.'

Pat Larry's face, as he looked up at his adversary, twisted into a leer of hatred. He crouched on his knees and hands then lurched to the side and stood up. He faced the butcher, his fists lifted in the manner of a pugilist and began to shift slowly about the bigger man.

'Right,' he hissed, 'let's see what a butcher who can carve poor helpless sheep into lumps of shit can do when faced with a real man. You and your rotten meat, you both stink like the stink ridin' the air up here.'

'Stop!' came a scream from the Captain, who still stood a little back from them both.

They hesitated, and turned towards him. Astonished, they saw he had his rifle raised and aimed at them, the barrel shifting slowly and steadily from one to the other.

'And don't think I won't use it. I'd be only too glad to use it, I can tell you. The first one of you who moves I'll shoot the balls off him, so help me God.'

Suddenly they heard a high-pitched howl from somewhere above and beyond the ridge, closer to them than they cared to know. They shifted uncertainly, drawing closer to one another in fear. The sound was eerie, a mixture of pain and sorrow and a certain rise of triumph in its long-drawn-out decrescendo.

'Jesus' – it was Casimir – 'it's the fuckin' bogman.'

Slowly the Captain shifted the barrel of his gun in the direction of the howl. The three of them stood petrified, wholly unable to move. The ridge was empty. A mist had come over it and was moving gradually about them.

'Where's Izabel?' Pat Larry whispered.

They realised the woman was nowhere to be seen. At the same time the density of the mist thickened about them and the sickening smell that filled the air seemed to be part of the very mist encompassing them about. There was a long silence between them. Slowly and certainly the fog thickened and held them. The silence was huge and oppressive, and the low moan of the wind filled up the dense fog.

'Where's Izabel?' Pat whispered again and came close to the Captain.

The Captain lowered his rifle slowly and gazed around as if he had just come out of a dream. 'Christ – what the fuck is going on?'

Casimir drew close to them both. There was silence between them, a wariness mixed with an acute sense of embarrassment. They could see only a few yards in front of them now, through the moving, shifting fog. As they stood there they heard the animal howl again, coming as if it were carried with the stench that floated on the mist. It seemed further away now, fading into the distance. It lasted only a moment but hovered, rising and falling in pitch with an uncanny, heart-rending music. The three men drew closer to each other until their bodies touched. Then there was silence again.

Suddenly the Captain screamed: 'Izabel! Izabel!' And then, more quietly: 'Was that Izabel screaming? She could fall over a cliff in this fog. Or down into a boghole. We must find her. Stick close now. We'll go on over the ridge.'

Cautiously, almost like children clinging to one another, they moved higher along the ridge. They called her name, screaming it out of their own dread and thrusting it against the blankness of the world about them. There were rocks rising like great animals from the earth, from the gullies and small valleys, the heather roots were thick and corded, ferns concealed damp patches of ground, the mosses and grasses were dense and cloying and here and there were long harsh arms of reaching brambles, thin and rough and grasping. They stumbled and cursed their way higher, their hearts pounding, fear holding them the way the fog had held them.

As they topped the ridge they could see that the fog was passing like a cloud from them. It grew thinner gradually, and the stench that accompanied it began to fade. The fog faded into tatters of itself, into wisps, then it was gone. They stood, waiting. Again and again they screamed out Izabel's name, but only a faint echo came back to them from the higher walls of the mountain, and the soft breathing of the fog and wind. Quickly the air cleared and they could see a small blanket of sunshine moving over the surface of the sea far below.

They waited, calling. Very soon the air was clear about them and they could see in every direction. There was no sign of the woman. The Captain grew frantic and set off hopelessly along the top of the ridge, calling and scrambling in every direction. For over three hours they raked the hillside, approached the edge of the cliffs and looked over. There was no trace of Izabel. She seemed to have vanished into air, the way the mist had vanished, the way the awful stench had left the valley lying in its own bewildered and bewildering calm.

For several days groups of men scoured the landscape, searching. A boat was sent out and it moved slowly and dangerously by the cliffs. There was no sign, no trace anywhere, of the woman. The mountain stood, silent, impassive, above all their efforts.

7

Footsteps. Heavy. Approaching her where she sat. Her whole body swaying in anticipation of capture. She drew away from the road, from the day, from time. Down deeper into the fortress she had built within herself. She knew its vastness, the massive storeys above her; beneath her, spaces, corridors, dark rooms with shut doors. An interior castle. Soul-house.

When she stood up it felt as if she had been under the weight of this house for ever. She did not dare begin to ascend the first stair-case which was wide enough for her to lie stretched out along its every step. It disappeared, turning gently into the darkness above. Everywhere there was silence, apart from the ponderous ticking of a grandfather clock in an alcove under the stairs. It was an uneasy silence, made the more so by her own fears and doubts that seemed to speak and whisper into the air about her, her weariness, her thirst, so that the very air in which she stood vibrated with the vibrations of her breathing life.

How greatly hindered is the inner life of a human being by the needs of the body.

The words seemed to come to her from the dust swirling in the pale light from an old window, as if all the motes had gathered themselves together to shape the phrase. And yet she knew she had spoken them out of herself, out of the store of wisdom that lay inside the castle through which she moved.

Somewhere, far away behind the walls and corridors of the great house, a door banged shut. She was startled. She could not be found in here, she must not be taken now. *Today a man is standing in this place, tomorrow he is gone.* Like a small blossom on a tall, spectacular cherry tree. *Who will notice? Or who will care?* She decided, quickly, and opened a small insignificant door in one corner of the great panelled hall.

It was dim inside, with crude cement steps leading immediately downwards, curving quickly away beneath her. *Act now, beloved soul, for you do not know the hour you will be taken.* She stepped into the dimness and shut the door quietly behind her. For a long time she stood, waiting for the wooden echoes to die away. Waiting for her eyes to get used to the dimness. Then she stepped down, the first step. There was a familiarity here, something about the plain, dull, whitewashed walls, the smoothed centre of the cement steps as she went down, the faint but certain light that should be coming from naked bulbs high on the whitewashed walls; but there were no bulbs, there was only the light. The familiarity, vague as it was, reassured her. Keeping her right hand close to, at times touching the wall, she went down, cautiously.

For a time the steps spiralled gently, the air grew chilly, but the light stayed constant. She was grateful for the silence here, a silence she could control should she stop the sound her shoes made on the steps, should she still her breathing. *You should place in its perspective your every thought and action as if this very day were to be your last.* Step after step after step. Down; down; down; regular, steady heartbeat.

Eventually she came down onto a level area, a small room without door or window, yet even here the dim light remained. Here, too, it was warmer. There was no issue. Only the steps back up to the hallway of the great house. There were no furnishings, the cement floor was clean, free of dust, free of the carcasses of flies or mice or beetles. Clean. Empty. White.

Once, while I was at prayer, I saw myself standing alone in a large field, and around me there was a crowd of people, hedging me in on every side. It seemed to me they were all carrying weapons with which they would attack me: lances, swords, daggers, rapiers. There was no way of escape for me without running the immediate risk of death, and I was quite alone, there was no one to take my part. I was in terrible spiritual distress and I did not know where to turn, when I raised my eyes to the heavens and saw my Christ — not in heaven, but far above me in the sky, holding out His hand to save me, encouraging me in such a way that I did not fear any more those people, and I knew they could do me no harm, try as they might.

She shook her head to clear the voices that she knew were not real, not living flesh and tissue, were her own voice, her own memories. Here, on the solid ground of her silence, her freedom, she was secure, and at peace.

Love bade me welcome but my soul drew back, guilty of dust and sin.

The only danger now would be from within her own soul, and if the Fiend himself should come, then she knew it would be the creation of her own life, no more, no less. She sat down on the concrete floor and folded her legs beneath her. *Very soon the end of your life will be at hand; you must consider, then, the state of your soul; for if you are not ready to die today, will tomorrow find you any the better prepared? Tomorrow is as uncertain as is your breathing; how can you hold onto tomorrow?* If she should succeed in preparing her soul, then she could rise, secure, into the day.

She closed her eyes. A gentle warmth seemed to suffuse her entire body. A blanket of peace about her. Her weariness eased. Her body felt light as a goldfinch's feather. She opened her hands where they lay on her knees and turned the palms upward toward the sky. *Yes, all is well, all shall be well, and all manner of things shall be forever well.* Thus. For a time. A short time.

And then she heard the door bang shut again and the sibilant slithering of footsteps descending the stairs towards her. The Fiend. She knew it. And breathed easily. Unafraid. She smiled inside her own darkness, and waited. *Who will remember you when you are gone? And who will pray for you? Act now, dear heart. For you do not know the hour of your death, nor do you know your state beyond the gates of death.* The words settled about the floor of her castle, comforting, identifiable, proven words. The footsteps had grown louder; they had stopped close to her. She heard a voice then, calling her, calling, calling ... She felt the touch of a hand upon her shoulder. She sighed. Waiting.

8

Joshua (Josh) MacLean realised he could squeeze no more sleep in behind his eyes. He got up. It had been a bad night, so bad it would become memorable. The glass of whiskey, growing to be a habit, had established that sense of pleasurable languor that promised a night's oblivion. But that benign lethargy was quickly dissipated by a visit to the bathroom. It was cold in the hallway, colder still in the bathroom. Josh closed the window tight against the cold, and against the white darkness that was hovering outside.

On the bathroom walls several woodlice crawled and he flicked them one by one onto the floor and trod on them; a shudder went through him as each body was crushed under his weight. In the bedroom it was coldest of all; the double bed was too large for a single body to warm it up and by one o'clock he was shivering and very much awake. He got up and spread his overcoat across the bed. Slowly warmth crept out of the night to seep into his body; he began to doze.

A tiny scrabbling on the wall brought him awake again. There was a mouse, active, the sounds magnified in the silence of the night. He tried to ignore the scraping, scratching sounds, but he could not; he reached out of bed for a slipper and flung it hard in the direction of the noise. There was silence for a moment; then the scraping and scratching began again. Josh sat up in bed, holding the winter coat against his chest; was there a God at all and if there was how could He be so harsh? The rustling sounds continued.

He got up, put the overcoat on over his pyjamas and went to get a mousetrap. Josh the mouse-killer. Braver than a hen. He put a piece of hard cheese on the hook and put the trap up against a gap between wall and floor. Then he got back into bed. The mouse kept on crumpling, scratching and eating newspapers in its chamber behind the wall for some minutes more; then there was silence. A dull stupor spread through Josh's brain. When the trap was sprung he came sharply awake, there was a click and a thud and he could hear the thump thump thump of a tiny body against the floor; then all was still, very, very still.

In the deep black pool of that night all he could hear now was the crackling of the winter darkness outside, and the buzz of loneliness in his head. He wondered if a mouse had indeed been caught, and if so, how – by the snout, or ears, or neck, or tail? He wondered if it had suffered; serves it right, then, for keeping him awake. He imagined the awful suddenness of the trap, the cheese, the temptation that had promised a rare delight, a gift, then – schwack! Pain and blood, agony and death; the terrible cheat of it, the betrayal, the cruelty. How all of life is a promise, drawing us on, for what? Slaughter, agony and death! Josh was wide, wide awake.

He got up again, put on the coat, put on the light; there was a mouse, lying under the wooden trap. Josh turned it over; a clean kill! He picked up the trap and the body; the tail hung down and swung as he walked; he went into the kitchen, opened the lid of the range and let the dead mouse drop into the dead fire. There was a stain of blood on the tip of the trap; he let the trap drop, too, into the range.

Back in bed he felt colder than ever. He put on a pair of socks and a jumper, sat for a while in the armchair and sipped another whiskey. Then he got back into bed and tried again; he was an Eskimo, wrapped up and fishing for sleep through a tiny hole in the ice. He was an explorer, huddling in his tent while the Himalayan winds screamed about him like a herd of abominable snowmen. The Yeti. Wolf packs prowling round the most intrepid explorer. Call of the wild. All that.

The cheese? What had happened the little bit of cheese he had left on the trap? The question bothered him, and he could not stop its scraping inside his head. He found the bit of cheese on the floor near the wall of the bedroom, took it out to the kitchen and dropped it after mouse and trap. It was just four o'clock. He boiled a kettle, made himself a strong hot toddy with lots of sugar. Then he sat up in bed, nursing the glass between his hands, sipping quietly. Feeling sorry for himself. It is sad for a man to sleep alone.

Now he dreaded more than ever the day ahead. How could he face into the alert cheerfulness of children in his classroom, their swept faces, their eager greetings, their pushing and shoving as they offered him their little pieces of news, their drawings, their colourings-in. He would be tired, quickly bored, querulous. He could so easily squash their little delights, their expectations, their innocence. Squash them, like woodlice under his boots. Thirty little boys he had, all clean of sin, their first confessions still months ahead, the sunshine and rhododendron day of their First Communions like a dream before them.

And in the evening he had promised Patty they would drive together back to the amethyst quarry at the foot of the mountain. As he sipped his warm drink, a small and different scratching began against the thin skirting board of his brain. Patty. She was young, yes, and pretty; and they had good times together. Yes. But she was not beautiful. Not – sexy. And she was so often ill. She could be demanding, would be . . . And if this was love, if this was to be his portion? Did he not deserve better? After all, wasn't he young and active, he had dreams, the world was bright and wide and there were places where song was king and life was rich and golden. Patty O'Higgins. The Captain's daughter. Dull, already hurt. And a small school down a ragged road where children, like the scarecrow fuchsia bushes near the shore, were happy simply to exist and to live out the seasons as they came and went. Without questioning them. Without demands. Bobbing like old currachs on the same old ocean.

Josh knew that right now he was deeply unhappy. Taut, and held in a trap of his own making.

He slept; at last; uneasily. It was after four thirty.

When they met that evening, Patty was taciturn and remote. Josh was tired. He picked her up in his car, a small yellow Beetle of which he was very proud. The Captain greeted him at the door and offered him a glass of wine. Nora was sitting in near darkness down in the living room. She called 'Bye, love' when she heard the door shut behind her daughter.

Josh drove in silence, back over the hill, down the long slope into the village. He suggested a drink in the Village Inn. Patty was willing but not eager; she drank a vodka and orange; Josh had a pint. In the pub they were quiet, just a few comments about weather, the fishing, the year. It was dusty and dim in the room, the barman desultorily wiping glasses and watching inside his own mind, one man sitting alone at the bar, his hands wrapped around his glass. Patty was abstracted and still. Pretty, yes, well-formed, though slight, her eyes the most beautiful he had ever seen, big, limpid, brown, unlocked. Once she drew in closer to him and held his arm and he was surprised, his hand quickly covering hers, his heart beating faster – with sympathy, he realised, rather than with love.

They drove on, back through the next small village and up the newly built road towards the bay. They stopped high on the side of the cliff, watching down over the bay where the water glittered in the late sunlight. Then they continued as far as the quarry. Josh parked the car high on a sward bank. They poked and pottered listlessly among the rocks a while. They found nothing. Not even one tiny shining gem among the tons of grey and sandy shale and stones of the quarry. Patty was dispirited, she complained of the cold. Josh was quiet, withdrawn, without ardour.

As a soft rain began to fall, coming in long ghostly swathes from the side of the mountain, they climbed back into the car and sat together, watching out through the quickly misted windows. For

Patty it seemed that this slow mist of rain was a blessing. Taking her in from the world. Cocooning her within the confines of the small car. Josh yawned heavily and leant back uncomfortably in his seat.

At last, out of the gloom and the silence of the evening, Patty turned towards him. 'Josh,' she said, very quietly. 'I know I'm not the most beautiful woman in the world, not the most full of animation and excitement; you must feel free to leave me, whenever you wish.'

Josh looked at her. Although she was answering his unspoken thoughts, he was astonished and distressed. There were the beginnings of tears in her eyes. He reached for her, quickly. 'Never, Patty, never! What makes you talk like that?'

She shrugged her shoulders and smiled at him, ruefully. 'I'm not well, Josh, you know that, and sometimes I think I never will be well. I don't want you to feel that you must tie your life to mine, just because you were kind enough to date me for a while. I'm very fond of you, Josh, but there's something − I don't know, something . . .'

'How is Nora?' Josh asked suddenly.

'She's the same, Josh, she's always the same. And sometimes I think that I'll be like that too, and it would kill me to think that I had laid such an awful burden on you.'

Josh protested vociferously, his handsome face urging itself towards compassion.

'If I ever thought that it was pity you felt for me, Josh, I think I would walk away from you at once. I could not take pity from you, I do not want pity, do you understand?'

He was unable to answer and she drew him across the seat towards her. They kissed, gently, on the mouth, and her small hands caressed his hair. He laid his head, then, on her breasts and she caressed him in the tiny misted cavern of the car while the world outside stirred uneasily. Josh closed his eyes and felt the gentle heaving of the young woman's breasts.

For some time they remained like that, peaceful, close, together. Two animals, young and unproven, their skins touching.

Then she spoke again, very softly, hesitantly. 'Would you like to touch my breasts, Josh?'

He sat up quickly, startled. He looked at her. She was shy, smiling towards him, her eyes large and clear, her lower lip trembling a little. Her innocence accused him at once of guilt and he was glad of the darkness of the car. Cautiously and awkwardly he reached his right hand towards her blouse and touched it. He held his hand against her left breast a moment, his stomach dry and tense, his penis already rising against him. He looked into her eyes again. She had closed them, lightly, and a peaceful smile was on her face.

'The other one too,' she whispered. She breathed deeply, sighing with the simple pleasure of it.

His hands moved with infinite care; he worked to contain the growing excitement within him, aware that there was something in this young woman that seemed to draw the very best from him, a tenderness, an anxiety to please and not to hurt. He too closed his eyes with the pleasure of the moment and when he opened them again her eyes were on him, her face beautiful in its gladness.

'You don't think I'm awful?' she asked him.

'Oh no,' he said, 'not at all. You're wonderful. Wonderful.' His own life lifted strongly towards her for the moment, protective, loving, even yearning.

As they drove back towards her home, Patty was watching up the mist-covered sides of the mountain. She could see sheep huddling against the wetness.

'I see the sheep are back on the mountainside, Josh. Things have been quiet for some time now.'

'Yes,' he answered. 'There's been no signs of trouble for a long time.'

She paused. 'Not since poor old Izabel disappeared up there,' she said at last. 'As if her disappearance satisfied the mountain. It's official now, Josh,' she added sadly. 'Her things, you know, the house in Dublin, all of that, her trunk. It seems she left everything she owned to a charity in Dublin. Just the house, really, and the furniture. I don't think she had much, in spite of what we all believed. But she left the trunk to me. Poor old Izabel. Imagine – that famous trunk, kept in storage for years. And it's supposed to be mine. I feel responsible, in a way, for her disappearance. Even after all these years I blame myself. Except, Josh, those pains were not in my imagination. I get them still, except now I can cope with them a little better. I will have a normal life, won't I, Josh? Won't I?'

He reached across to her and held her hand. 'Yes, Patty, of course you will. Of course you will.'

The Captain felt good. Very good. He was a gamecock, his spurs sharp, the whole of the yard shimmering in homage before him. He must do something, something to show his prowess in life, something of which he himself would be proud, something of which poor Nora would be proud.

Nora was in hospital. Having tests. Poor Nora, how she suffered. He bought her a washing machine, a new one. And a cooker. Taking the old pre-war range away. Proudly he stood over the men as they heaved and carted and installed. Patty painted the kitchen a bright and warming yellow.

The Captain took the two wool mats from the parlour and put them in the washing machine. Eagerly he watched in through the porthole as they spun and stopped and spun again. Oh he would be famous in this house, lighting a fire of joy in his wife's strained face when she walked in the door.

He grew impatient. The mats kept spinning. Tomorrow she would be home. The day was turning dark. It might rain. How on earth would he ever get them dry and stretched out in all their beauty on the parlour floor before her?

'It takes about an hour and a half, Dodgie,' Patty laughed at him. 'Mamsa used to do them in the lake in twenty minutes.'

'About another half an hour, so.' He watched out the window towards the wood. 'Won't take me long to wait a half an hour.'

A first few drops of rain tickled the outside of the window. The machine whirred and purred. It squirted water out a pipe and away down the drain. It spun and spun. It shook, dancing lightly where it stood. The Captain was startled. Then it stopped.

They were wet when he took the mats out of the hold of the machine. It was pouring outside. His body felt heavy with disappointment. He would hang them in the shed outside and hope they would dry overnight.

As he searched for somewhere to hang the mats, the Captain

noticed the old mangle Nora had used years ago to wring the water from her washing. He hoisted and hefted it out from all the junk and stood it, a Trojan Horse, in the middle of the floor. His God was kind. He would have the stuff dry for Nora.

He put the first thick mat into one side of the mangle and pulled and dragged the end of it between the two rollers. He grasped the handle and began to turn it. The mat moved reluctantly into the grip of the rollers, moved, and stuck. The Captain strained and heaved but the stuff was too thick to pass through. He tried to turn the handle the other way. It would not budge. Over an hour he spent, pulling and turning and heaving; the sweat stood out on his forehead and ran in tiny streams down the undergrowth of his chest. Pieces of wool came away in his fingers. He began to curse.

Then he took a screwdriver and opened the sides of the old mangle, separating the rollers, withdrawing the weary mat. He held it up before him; it was ruined, the wool dirtied with oil, torn, shredded, ripped, like a sheep that had stood an hour in a storm and then fallen into a drain. Was there no God? the Captain asked the walls of his shed, no justice, no caring, no peace?

He brought the second mat back into the kitchen. If he had the old range, now, the mat would dry before its perpetual, delicate heat. He turned on the oven of the new gas cooker and put the mat inside. He closed the door and stood back. Ten minutes, he reckoned, ten minutes would see it dry enough to put beneath the iron. The rain thumped and shouted against the window. Soon the Captain noticed a strange, not unpleasant smell upon the air. Then small signals of smoke began to force their way out of the oven. He dived. Broken. Betrayed. Bereft. And down in the parlour two patches of lighter colour were to be seen where the mats had rested for so many years.

Josh was strutting famously about his little kingdom. His subjects were small ten-year-olds, for the most part eager, the world before them, all knowledge waiting, like a tree bursting with ripe apples to be picked. The walls were in bloom – pictures, charts, maps, histories, languages.

Animals. The elephant. Hannibal. The horse. The Trojan war. Josh was in bloom. Love-drunk. Male. Self-conscious.

'The heroes of an early war, boys, proud as Punch! Aeneas, Hector, Paris, Troilus, and all the heavy warriors of Greece, loud in conclave, male, aggressive, tall. All of them real he-men, muscle-men, clumps! Agamemnon, Nestor, Ulysses, Menelaus, sucking glory, boys, from the flesh of war, chewing on the bones of the hapless dead, looking for marrow.'

The boys glanced at each other, grimaced, put their heads down. Adults!

Dingoes. Dodos. Dromedaries. Ducks.

'Our living friends, boys, the kingdom of the animal. Beside us, their world, yet impenetrable. Different. Other.'

Birds. The curlew. The tree creeper. The kingfisher. Crow.

'Alien to us, boys, flight, impossible for us without the lumbering thrust of the engine.'

The wolf. *Lupus*. Romulus and Remus. Wolfhound. She-wolf. Dog.

'The wolf. *Canis lupus*. Dog. Hunter. A beautiful animal. Misunderstood. A scapegoat. They talk of lust, of the wolf whistle, the beast of waste and desolation. Not so, boys, not so. The twelve days of Christmas, blessed days, are the wolf's days. Holy creatures, boys, misunderstood and hunted down.'

A hand in the air.

'MacNamara?'

'The men say the wolf is the devil's dog, sir.'

'They say that, MacNamara, yes they do, because they do not understand the wolf. Look at all the Indians who loved, even worshipped the wolf, great warriors all, generous spirits, fighting for the survival of their tribes. Little Wolf, *Cheyenne*. Wolf Lying Down, *Kiowa*. Mad Wolf, *Seminole*. Wolf Orphan, *Blackfoot*. Wolf Face, *Apache*. Do you not thrill at the names, boys? *Theriophobia*, there's a word. *Theriophobia*. Fear of the beast. Fear of ourselves, fear of what we know is wicked in our own hearts.'

Puzzled faces.

Soon, a hand.

'Dempsey?'

'Sir, was it a wolf done in the sheep on the mountain?'

'A wolf, Dempsey? No, no, our wolves have long been done to death themselves. There are no wolves in Ireland any more.'

'Was it a werewolf, so, sir?'

Josh paused and looked at the serious face, felt the intensity in the air about the other boys, looking up, alert.

'Lycanthropy? No, Dempsey, no. Lycanthropy. We are all werewolves, all of us, when we know the wickedness that grows and festers deep within and when we can yet walk and live with one another. In the dark ages they hunted witches, wizards, were-wolves, because the times were dark. Now the times are bright, we know everything, we are not barbarians, we . . .'

'What was it so, sir, done in the sheep?'

'And Izabel O'Higgins?' Another voice, insistent, sharp.

'If I knew the answer to that wouldn't I be famous? I don't know, boys, I don't know. Some misfortune hit poor Miss O'Higgins. Some hole, or pit, or cliff. And some class of wild dogs took the sheep. So they say. Now, back to the lesson in hand. Animals, the horse. *Hippus*. The Trojan Horse. Remember? The shire, the Clydesdale, the hackney, the Shetland, the Cleveland Bay . . .'

It was deep winter. The nights were long, dank and cold. The mists were moving across the island like spirits, silent, blind, relentless. And as they passed they reached their long, chilling fingers through every crevice and chink and crack in the walls of shed, barn and house, whispering further into the warmest corners of the homes, drawing their nails over the flesh of the living, and of the dying.

Casimir Conlon, grown ponderous and heavy with the passing of the years, sat in his kitchen, his mind sodden with boredom. He had let the fire die away, it was a grey-black mess in the grate and the only light left in the room was the tiny perpetual lamp under the Sacred Heart. Casimir's eyes were growing dim from seeing nothing in life ahead. His soul had grown leaden from loneliness. Grit on the heart. Wet sand along the brain.

He sat, leaning back on his wooden chair, his legs stretched out in front of him, ungainly, careless of himself and of the world. His thoughts floated on nothing, like tiny tufts of thistledown floating over the reaches of a bog. His eyes, fixed vacantly on the wall before him, were glazed with boredom. Soon he would sleep, soon, when the weariness of his body grew too heavy to support against the darkness of the night.

Then, suddenly, out of the black reaches of the night, he was certain he heard the sound. At once, though there had been years between, he recognised it and sat chilled, in a darkness buzzing with his terror. His hands on his knees. Gripping. His eyes alert again. And wild. A far, low-pitched, inhuman, moan. Or a rising wind perhaps? His hands relaxed their clutch. It could be the first heaving groans of a midnight wind. He strained to hear. It came again, no nearer, higher in pitch, short, almost a cry. A keening. Almost a call.

Without moving his head Casimir looked towards the light switch near the door. It was scarcely visible in the darkness of the room. He was scared to move lest out of the darkness something should grip him before he could get to the light. He was frightened to reveal his existence to the night. He sat on, frozen into his chair. His heart thumped wildly.

When the kitchen door began to open, Casimir rose as if a slow spring inside him had begun to uncoil, forcing him up in spite of himself. His wooden chair fell over and clattered loudly on the kitchen flags. There was no escape. His body had grown cold, as cold, he knew, as if it had lain for days under the soil. Chilled. Frozen.

Casimir rushed suddenly, with a loud shriek, and switched on the light.

Pee-Wee was standing in the half-open doorway, grey-faced, her grey-white hair thin and ugly and unkempt, falling about her face like wet strips of paper. Her nightdress, a pale green colour, reached to the floor and the top was open, revealing the shrivelled flesh of her neck. She had not been out of bed for fifteen years.

'Help me, Casimir,' she cried in a shrill, trembling voice. 'Help me. The banshee ... I've heard the banshee. It's for me. The banshee. It's my turn ...'

Casimir stood petrified in the middle of the room. His mother seemed to have grown taller, as if she hadn't straightened out her body in years. He stood, his mouth open, his big hands half-raised in defence, his body tensed toward the ghost and turned, at the same time, toward some alley of escape. The old woman was already looking far beyond this pathetic man in her path, looking into whatever vast abyss only she could see and that had opened up, at last, before her. Forcing her, after years, out of the bed, out of the room, back towards the world where life still carried on.

She spoke again, her voice cracked now and low, as if a different existence already spoke out of her. Her hands were stretched out towards him. She tried to move into the kitchen, into his presence, into the light, but all she could achieve were jerky movements, from her hips and the upper parts of her body.

'Help me, for God's sake, help me, can't you help me?' She was whining now, whining. 'I can't move. I'm stuck to the ground,' and she reached towards him again, stretching, her hands shaking, like brittle branches in a rough wind. 'I can't move, Casimir. My hand, it's covered in leaves, old brown leaves, there are birds in my hair, and they're pecking at my skull. They're inside my skull, Casimir, help me, help me, heeeeelllllllp . . .'

Her voice rose to a wail. She screamed again, 'Casimir!', her whole body swaying and trembling and straining towards him. And then it stopped. The voice uttered no more sounds, the trembling ceased, her eyes were open, wide open, her mouth, old and ugly and dried up, open, too. She just stopped. Dead. And stood. Like a tree. Gnarled. Hard-skinned. Dead.

For how long she stood like that Casimir could never tell. He stood too, helpless, terrified beyond movement. Beginning to sense the absence. The darkness beyond the walls. The spaces.

Slowly then, without a sound, the dead woman fell forward onto the kitchen floor, stiff and straight, her head thumped against the hard flags of the floor. That sound above all made him move. He screamed, a scream of anger at the world that had delivered that sight to his life, a scream of terror, knowing the malevolent presence of death chilling the roots of his hair, and then he rushed to gather up the dead weight of his mother as if she were a baby, carrying her back down the short hallway to her room.

He laid her on the bed, arranged her hands over her chest and hung her Rosary about the fingers. He put his own fingers on her eyelids and pressed them shut. He closed the mouth and raised the head on the pillow so that her chin rested against her bosom, keeping the mouth closed. He arranged the few wisps of hair over the purple weal on her brow. He straightened the bedclothes, opened the small window and drew the curtains. He listened for a while, waiting to hear the long triumphant howl of the banshee. But he heard nothing, only the faintest whisper of the passing winds. He turned her mirror to the wall, dropped to his knees beside the bed and searched frantically for some words that might form a prayer for her, and for himself.

A trunk was delivered to the house at the crossroads. Patty had it carried, at once, down to her room. There it stood, big and solid and real, all of a life, and nothing. It was dark blue, with brass hinges and brass bars and bolts. Hooped over with neat binding rods. A treasure chest, from the past, from the unreal world of yarns and wars and wonders.

She sat on the bed a while and looked at it, as if expecting it to speak or move or reveal itself to her without her asking. The long morning emptiness deepened; somewhere beyond the house a dog barked and the heavy air seemed to shiver in response. The moment was tense with absence, sprung with the name, *Izabel; Izabel Ingrid O'Higgins.*

Patty sat a while longer, her heart filled with sorrow and memories. She got up then, the springs of the bed scringing a little under her. She took the key from the envelope taped firmly to the side of the trunk and put it in the lock. It turned easily, with a grateful sigh. She lifted back the heavy lid.

Lying on top of a jumble of clothes was a thick brown envelope, tied tightly with rubber bands. She took that out and held it a moment, wondering; then she left it down on her dressing table. The image of Dickens's Miss Haversham floated into her mind as she touched the clothes. One by one she took them out, unfolded them, and laid them on the bed. There were dresses and slips, old-fashioned, off-white, grey or dull cream, with lace and filigree, elaborate button and ribbon fastenings. Smelling of the mothballs placed between and among them. A little soiled. Delicate.

Underneath the dresses were two heavy woollen dressing gowns; there were cardigans and three pairs of slippers. All of these she laid on the bed, slowly, with reverential care. Somewhere in the house a door banged and she was startled, as by ghosts. She could see sheets folded and laid neatly towards the bottom of the trunk and on top of them were objects wrapped in layers of newsprint. These she unwrapped with extreme care, placing each object on the floor, smoothing out the papers as well as she could and laying them on the rug. Cups. Saucers. Plates. A teapot. Jug. Coffee pot. Cutlery. All dull and uninteresting and commonplace. The fathomable accidents of a life. Ignorable. She wondered why all this had been done, the packing of all these items of dullness and uninterest.

A small brown cardboard box.

Shoes. Some underwear. Pillowcases.

She lifted the last sheet from the floor of the trunk with a sense of deep disappointment. So that was all. The dullest items laid by in case – in case of what? Set apart and held, paid for as if she had no space for them among all the rooms and bibelots of her house in Dublin. Set apart in case of what? Of war? Exile? Refuge? To start again on a life with at least these items for hold?

All the stuff seemed old and fragile and unhealthy and Patty knew they would never be used again. One by one she replaced them in the trunk, the sheets, the dresses, the shoes, the newspapers and tissue papers, the little army of mothballs. She closed down the lid of the trunk with a sense of sadness. She had not known what to expect, so what she felt was some vague empathy; perhaps she had hoped for treasures from an exotic imagination, invoking magic or mystery, or even distant places, dreams. But all that was here was heaviness, decay, the drab and dull things of a drab and dull life.

She carried the cutlery and cups to the kitchen and left them out on the sideboard. Perhaps they could be given away. If anyone cared for them. Travellers. Beggars. Children, even, setting them up for cock-shots along a wall. She touched, for a moment, the sunshine of the morning, watching the motes of dust in the sun's rays that came through the escallonia leaves onto the ground, then she went slowly back to her room. There was the small cardboard box. And the brown paper package. Something possible still.

She tore the tape off the box and opened it. It was small, hardly bigger than a cigarette box; it had a postmark outside: London, 29 March 1950. The name and address had been torn off.

Medals. A slip of paper stating: 'The Under-Secretary of State for War presents his compliments and by Command of the Army Council has the honour to transmit the enclosed Awards granted for service during the war of 1939–45.' A slip of paper, formal, impersonal, going yellow and fraying along the folds.

Patty turned the slip over. It described the medals enclosed, with their ribbons. The 1939–45 Star, tarnished and heavy, and the ribbon, dark blue, red and light blue in three equal vertical stripes. 'This ribbon is worn with the dark blue stripe furthest from the left shoulder.' The Africa Star, ribbon pale buff, with a central vertical red stripe and two narrower stripes, one dark blue, and the other light blue. The Italy Star, the Defence Medal, the War Medal. Their ribbons. Their silent testimonial. Patty wondered what they had meant to Izabel, if they were all those years had left her, how much of pain, horror and death had gone into the creation of these small shapes of metal.

Patty held each medal in her hand and placed the ribbon against it. Then she took all five and held them, closing her eyes and hearing the guns, the cannons, the cries, the screams. . . Aircraft droning overhead, dispensing horrors. The grinding advance of bone-crushing tanks, that deadly finger pointing, and spouting death. She opened her eyes at once and the medals lay in their quiet presence, heavy and old and dulled. Witnesses. Izabel amongst all that horror. Patty sighed and put them back in the box, then left it in the top drawer of her dressing table. Tangible souvenirs from a life. Valour. Bravery. Service. And sacrifice.

She picked up the envelope and took the rubber bands off, one by one, delaying the opening of this final package. It was a large envelope folded in two. She opened it. There was a bundle of letters inside, all held together by one more rubber band. Brown. Twisted and twisted firmly about them. Letters. On a fine paper, light blue, woven, rich. The first one dated September 1945, the last one July 1946. The handwriting strong at first, and flowing, neat and wonderfully legible, although the ink had begun to fade from black to a dark grey. Patty sat on the bed with a sense of pleasurable expectation. She smoothed the first letter out and began to read.

My dearest Izabel,

So often, these times, I think of you, your fine, tender hands, your kind, lovely face, your care of me, your ministrations. The pains continue, as you said they would. They are intermittent, and I anticipate a difficult winter. But for me that terrible war was over the day I woke to your presence beside me. Do you think of me at all now? Will you write to the address I will give you at the end of this letter. Write discreetly, c/o Mrs Branson. She knows me. She will be discreet as well.

Juliet and the children crowd me. In body. In space. You crowd my thoughts and my affections. I hurt, Izabel, working to conceal ... I give, as excuse, my pains and sufferings and I have a room to myself where I sleep, apart from Juliet. I am wholly at one with myself. Wholly clear as to what my life must be. I will be true, Izabel, in spite of all, I will be true – to you, my dearest, until we can be together once again.

Please do not complain or make any manner of a fuss should the little shipment I have sent reach you. Take the things as kisses, embraces, tokens of love that would be much greater if only I could be forever with you. You shall truly kill me if you do not accept, and enjoy these things.

They, at least, will be near you. Holding you. And that, for the moment, must be my joy.

My love.
Write.
G.

Patty searched for the address the letter promised. There was no sign of it. She put this first letter down on the bed; the paper of the next was of a fine cream weave, the ink was coloured lavender, the folds were carefully made.

Darling,

Your letter today gave me such joy only the angels who
were witness to the Resurrection would have understood!
Out of my gloom and the darkness of my days, a vital
flower! Thank you for it. You have entered my soul and
taken root there and you have grown into a great flower of
passion. Like a sudden lotus in the desert. Our desert, my
love. I pine for you. I suffer agonies for your presence.

Juliet has taken to haranguing me now, day by day by
day. She says I exaggerate my pains and am neglecting her
and the children. She is right, of course, but what am I to do?
How can I look at candles in the gloom when the sun is
burning brighter than ever before the eyes of my soul?

Jennie – Mrs Branson – handed me your letter without a
word. But she knows my life. And I could not wait. I opened
it before her, my hands shaking so that the envelope fell onto
the ground before me. And my face must have shone like the
daystar when I read your word: BELOVED. You spoke that
word into my fevers in the tent in Bouktoub-bel-Ouhran
and it brought me then out of the hell of suffering into the
paradise of hope. As it does now, once again. Thank you for
this gift, this treasure. I picked up the envelope with as much
reverence as if it were a gem; I keep envelope and letter next
my heart, and will do so, always.

I entreat you, dearest . . . I entreat you. Do not fight with
me on this. I would do more, give up life itself, should it
bring us both together. No, I have said nothing to Juliet, not
to anyone, and Jennie Branson simply turned her head away
and allowed me my space to breathe in. But can I stand it?
Can I dissimulate much longer? Is it fair to you, or to Juliet?
Is it fair to me? And must not God Himself see that you and I
belong together? He will forgive me anything. Because it is
love. Love. Do not fight with me on this. Tell me you will
agree and at once I shall step forward and release my soul
from its terrible bondage. Juliet, too, will know release. And
the children.

Respond, dearest, and say yes. Soon, soon, soon. That I may come to you.

My heart's desire.

G.

Patty gazed for a moment out the window without seeing anything. The faded piece of paper was trembling in her hands. Precious, living, warm. With caution she set it down on top of the first one. Reverently. To the third. Blue again, black ink, the writing still fine and strong.

28 OCTOBER
LUTON

Dearest,

Do not berate me for the gifts. They are only my arms reaching for you, to embrace you. They are my thoughts, longing to be with you, in your company. I have wealth, and to spare. I owe you my life, my life, and you must live forever surrounded by my care, if not my arms. I shall be in London on the 5th November. 4 o'clock I shall see you! How my soul and body sing with joy at the prospect of it.

My love. All, all my love.

G.

The next letter was on a plain white paper, unlined, covered on both sides, ink showing through, and the writing moved like a river, flowing but unsteady, as if the banks that should have been there had burst and allowed the torrent too much space to turn in.

6 NOVEMBER
HOTEL CLARISSA
LONDON

My dearest, dearest, dearest!

Your message! It was like stepping out on firm ground and having it explode under my feet. Like the war all over again.

Only worse.

What fears you have, my dearest love! Can you not put them all away from you? What are they, compared with love? With our love. Love alone will conquer fear. It is greater than all, than you, or me, than us both. Love has set the heart racing within me and only love can lay it back to rest. Having saved my life are you now about to kill me? London, how I hate it now; in all its sadness, its rubble, its broken bones, its agonies from the years of bombing. Yesterday it was a heavenly garden for me, filled with flowering aisles and scented bowers, yesterday I was entering through the golden groves. And now, now it is dust and decay, it is sewer and stone and I cannot bear it.

I will be here again six days before Christmas. This time, my dearest love, your scruples and hesitations, your fears and anxieties, please, PLEASE! put them aside, just for once, for one day. It will be Christmas, free Christmas once again, and we will be able to celebrate our love, together, we will celebrate peace, and freedom, a new year, the future.

Do not think I am so blind as not to understand your fears, do not ever, ever think so. But our love, our love must overcome all that.

Oh let the new year be OUR year. Write. Let the new year . . .

The words ended suddenly the way a river will disappear over a cliff. Patty's body was in agitation. The letter trembled violently in her hand. She set it down with the others and got up to pace the room a while. Outside the world turned as it always turns, imperceptibly, inexorably, indifferent. From somewhere beyond the house there came the faint sound of hammering but it echoed strangely where she sat. As if this room were the real world and that, with the hammering sounds, was a world of spirits. Yet in her room, about the trunk, there seemed to hover such an air of sadness and emptiness, of loss and timelessness, that Patty shivered, as if chilled. She felt unable to continue to read. The corner of a cardigan appearing from the top of the trunk filled her with sorrow for the life that had been Izabel's. The loss. The fears. The pain somewhere permanently in her soul that had kept her solitary, isolated, shunned. She flicked quickly through some of the letters and picked up the last one. It had no address, no date. It was on a page torn roughly from some copybook, a child's exercise book, and the writing was almost that of a child, careless, rambling, loose.

My dear Izabel,

You have not written. I know now that all is lost. I have settled into a dull lethargy of continuous pain. I have regretted that I ever woke from my wounds into your lovely presence. I have regretted that I came back to life at all. Day does not seem to follow day any more, my life just oozes away. I can find no interest in anything about me. I regret being rescued from the field of war. I have suffered in a more terrible war. I can no longer believe in the truth of love. I can scarcely believe now that you exist, that you ever existed, that anything other than pain has ever existed. There is no God. There is only pain. And yet I have known love and I have seen what life could have been. I understand, believe me, I do understand. I cannot accept your fears, but you know I understand them. Thank you for your words, your wishes, your advice. We are moving from here and will be in Italy by September. The business takes care of itself now, without me. Juliet is convinced that my nerves were shattered during the war and has become more kind to me than I can cope with. My children treat me from a distance, as if I were some fool, some stranger with whom they do not care for commerce. I have laid down my arms, I have laid aside all my dreams. In Italy, I know, I will achieve an evening calm. I expect no more. I will accept less. Know that I will always love you. Always. Love me, too. Perhaps there is a better world. (I think we fought for such a world.) Perhaps you and I will meet in a better world. It is to that possibility, God help me, that I shall now look forward.

May your God, dear Izabel, show kindness towards you for the sacrifices you have made.

Forever yours.
G.

The letters made a small heap on the eiderdown. Patty put the final one on top and then picked them all up, slowly, and put them back in the envelope. Her body hung heavily. Izabel was there with her in the room as she had never been before. Patty alone had been admitted to her heart, a world of love and passion, of pain and dreams, of repression and loss. The great sore in the human heart. She felt humbled, strengthened, too, to face her own future.

She got the Captain to heave the trunk out to the ash pit behind the sheds. Inside the trunk, somewhere in its very heart, among all the clothes and sheets and pillows, she had placed the bundles of rolled-up newspapers. She found them, and the tissues, and she poured paraffin over them and set them alight. Then she put back the rest of the clothes in the trunk and moved away a little.

Quickly the flames devoured all that was left of this life, silently at first, black and grey smoke rising slowly, almost reluctantly into the noon sky. As the timber frames caught fire, and the canvas sides, there began a loud crackling, as of rapid, important chattering. Patty came as close as she could and threw the large brown envelope of Izabel's letters into the heart of the fire. The flames seemed to burn with a brilliant flame for a moment. Soon she was able to come behind the trunk and, with the handle of a rake, she pushed the lid shut. Smoke billowed again and then the lid, too, took fire. Very soon only a blackened wire frame stood like a skeleton among the flames, the smoke and the sparks. And then it, too, collapsed on the small mattress of ash; Patty imagined the sound of its collapse was a soft sigh of release.

Every few days the Bomber Tuite drove his cattle up to the lower pastures of the mountain. Mike-Joe Tuite was a big man, big and slow, his complexion darkened from the heather winds and from his own innermost thinking. He walked with a lurching, uneven gait, like that of his lumbering cattle, every step considered to see if it were worth the effort, every greeting on the way a grunt of complaint. His lumpish stick was thumped off the dirt-caked rumps of the cows with a dull finality.

The Bomber's home was a stable, where he lived alone among mysteries never probed by neighbour or inspector. He sat in the early evenings, smoking, his thoughts worthy of being organised into a system to deaden the rushing optimism of the twentieth century. But he had not passed beyond sixth class in primary school and so his thoughts moved hither and yon, blown by the winds that veered in every direction off the changeable ocean.

The Bomber's dog, Prince, was wild, given to growling and baring his teeth. Faithful of days, he was the Bomber's one and only certain companion in life. The dog, one eye brown and one eye grey, his fistful of cows, and above all his sheep loitering on the high slopes of the mountain, were all of life to Mike-Joe 'the Bomber' Tuite. And the darker corners of the pub on winter evenings, and the relief of near drunkenness.

He closed the entrance gate to his lower field and began the slow drift up towards the higher slopes. He whistled the dog through his teeth and laughed when he saw the animal's delight as it bounded over the marshy ground, the mosses, skutch grasses, bogholes, scraws. The Bomber thumped his way after the dog, his wellingtons sucking and splooshing in the wet, his lumpish stick providing little support over the too-soft ground. But the sun shone brightly, the year was young, there was the sharpness of living in the clear air.

The Bomber Tuite climbed today without thought, his mind an almost perfect *tabula rasa*, his body intent on the ground, on his breathing, on his surest path. As he rose the world began to lay itself out in wonder behind and below him; but the Bomber Tuite did not turn; he had been this way often enough before. He had observed the world and placed it in its necessary position in his mind where it lay with the price of stout-and-chaser, the woe of the dead-and-unbaptised, the music of long sunsets and the existence of edible flowers. High up to his right he could see his dog; Prince was already keen to the task, brown eye on his master, pale grey eye towards the mountain.

Prince stopped then, all at once, by a corner of mountainside carved by the Atlantic winds into a miniature turf bank. The dog sniffed at a piece of heather and his ears went flat against his skull. He growled, a low, long growl, and the hair along his spine seemed to stiffen. He set off cautiously, without looking back, nose to the earth, following.

'Here, Prince! Prince!' the Bomber called, half-heartedly, and the dog ignored him. The Bomber roared: 'Prince! Come back here, you dirty fuckin' whure!'

The dog did not hesitate for a moment. This was new, this was something the Bomber did not like; he sensed that the dog was going to bring this day into some new area of experience, round some corner where he did not think he wanted to venture. He whistled, three times, the special whistle that ought to have unleashed his dog towards the rounding down of his sheep. Prince kept his nose to the ground and moved at a faster pace, his belly almost rubbing the earth, and disappeared amongst the higher ridges and the boulders.

'The dirty, rotten whure of a baste,' muttered the Bomber, who began to pant as he tried to catch up a little on the dog.

The reaches of the mountain's flank rose at that point to a ridge, then dropped sharply to a valley and the dark waters of a lake, a narrow strip of land, and then another fall towards the sea. The dog had disappeared over the ridge in spite of the Bomber's repeated and irritated whistling. Higher up, to the right, the mountain rose to a flat top; to the left it rolled slowly away then rose again towards the higher reaches.

'Dirty pest. Dirty buggerin' pest.'

The Bomber heard a fierce growling that rose suddenly to a snarl and then a high-pitched barking that was cut off almost at once in a terrible animal scream. Then there was silence. The Bomber stopped, fear striking him for the first time. He glanced around, anxiously; the world about him was empty; there were no birds in the sky, no scald-crows, no gulls, no pipits. Everything was silent except for the wind shushing about the headlands and brushing through the heathers at the top of the ridge. The Bomber felt cold, though he was sweating from the climb. He wiped his brow with the back of his left hand. All that had ended, he thought, years ago. He whistled again, once, sharply. He found he was holding his lumpish stick, now, the way you would hold a weapon. He moved upwards, slowly, towards the ridge.

When he topped the ridge, the northeastern slopes of the mountain were at his feet, and the great stretches of Blacksod Bay opened out in the glory of sunshine to the silver shimmer of the horizon. Below him the ground fell steeply in ridges of heathers, grass and ferns to the edge of a precipitous cliff overhanging the lake. Far below, the lake was black and still and beautiful. Beyond it he could see the lower cliffs that fell to the beach where the sea was breaking softly. He could have been the only man moving through the first days of creation, up there, alone with the invisible God, and faced with demanding, inexorable beauty.

'Fucking baste,' the Bomber said, though there was no trace of the dog. He gazed up the rough slopes to his right, calling the dog's name, whistling. Fear kept growing in him as he worked his way, with extreme caution, down towards the cliff top. He clung with one hand to the tough stems of the heathers and the clumps of hardy grasses until he was able to look out over the cliff top and down towards the lake far below. On a ledge some twenty feet beneath him he saw the dog, lying among mosses and ferns. He called him, gently, but there was no stir from the animal. The Bomber looked up quickly, as if he had sensed a presence somewhere above him. Watching. But he saw nothing. The skin on the back of his neck had chilled.

He left his stick down beside a rock and began to slide-climb towards the ledge below. It was dangerous, his life depended on the slow, perfect moves he made. He was muttering to himself, intent on his safety. He pressed his big body into the slope that was not yet sheer. The earth was damp, the slope on this side rarely touched by the sun. There were tiny rivulets of water dripping from fern and moss but the ground was firm enough to hold him. He reached the ledge. The dog was strangely crumpled. With a sudden surge of sorrow he reached towards the black shape to touch it. At once he saw its head had been torn from its neck. The grass was soaked in blood. The side of the dog had been ripped open as if a sharp knife had been snagged along it and the soft whites and pinks and purples of its innards were hanging out.

The Bomber screamed. He clung quickly to the mountainside lest the terror of the sight precipitate him into space. Again he felt that quick chill across the back of his head and neck and a cold tremor of fear weighed on his shoulders. He looked up quickly as if he felt the power of eyes upon him from some part of the slopes above. He could see nothing. He lay still against the face of the mountain for a while, watching, breathing deeply. Nothing stirred. Nothing.

In a quick fit of rage and unknowing he put his right foot in under the splayed, headless body of his dog and jerked it outward into the air. It fell with unnerving silence, down, down, and down until he heard its body thump against rocky ground far below at the edge of the lake. He must get back up now, safely, take care, he told himself, take care now, infinite care. He gripped hard on the heathers, he found a foothold, he moved upward, step after step, concentrating all his being on every tiny move. He came up to the rock where he had left his stick. Only now did panic seize him and he began to clamber, awkwardly, slithering and sobbing, back to the top of the ridge. Unmanned. He, Mike-Joe Tuite, slobbering and unmanned. His clothes were wet and dirtied, his great man's body heaved with sobs, his big tanned face was quivering with shock. He crossed the ridge and began to run down the slope, back towards the lower pastures and the village. The warm sun bathed him again. The view of the whitewashed houses of the village steadied him. He stopped. He felt foolish.

'Fuck it!' he said out loud. And he turned back to face the ridge.

The world was empty now of his dog and he felt real sorrow and amazement. A quick covering of the sun by clouds sent a shiver of darkness across the flanks of the mountain. Then it struck him: he had not seen any of his sheep up there, or any other sheep. Not one. Not on any slope, or in the valley beyond, nor down by the lake. Was it starting up again? The threat, the dread, the unknowing? Now, with real decision, the Bomber turned back towards the village, and he walked and ran by turns, glancing up often and uneasily towards the ridge, as if he were being followed, his lumpish stick gripped tight as a cudgel in his fist.

Startling how a perfectly normal morning – gentle sunshine, the threat of rain, the cat stretching herself beside the wall, hens murmuring and shifting easily among gravel paths – can swell suddenly until it explodes into shards. How the night before had been so normal, the fire banked down, the doors locked and checked, the lights put out in order; all the normal sounds of doors, taps, toilet flushing; how silence had settled in then, darkness, and healing sleep.

But, imperceptible as the precise moment of the tide's turning, a threshold had been crossed. The Captain found Nora crumpled on the scullery floor, cold, still, face downward.

He came down the stairs, humming and fumbling as usual. He had washed, dressed, freshened himself. As usual. A certain lightness in the step. In the mind. He came along the hallway, admired again the diamonds of coloured light from the front-door panels shimmering on the tiles. He opened the door into the kitchen. The table was set for breakfast, three places, cups, saucers, plates and cutlery. Breakfast-room silence. Sunlight slanting across the table. One of Nora's slippers on the floor near the shut scullery door. The air tainted with the sweet-sour smell of gas.

In that long moment the Captain knew everything about Nora with absolute certainty. He knew her pain and darkness, he sensed the pale grey colouring of her life grow rapidly to an unbearable purple, he saw her hands that had clutched frantically at the world relax suddenly, and let go. And in that moment, in his own way, the Captain died.

Already he was feeling sick, his lungs protesting, his whole body out of tune. He moved swiftly. Somewhere in the dim landscape of his mind he saw a woman's shape, he was standing, small and alone, in a bathroom, lifting a bottle with something like lemonade in it and this well-dressed young woman came running up the stairs and in through the open door of the bathroom and knocked the bottle out of his hands. Smashing it against the tiles. The loud, sharp jaggedness of breaking glass. He opened the scullery door, flinging it back against the wall of the kitchen. At once he rushed and threw wide the scullery window, noticing, in his distress, a sparrow bathing itself in dust by the wall of the pine grove opposite. It was a detail that burned itself into his mind until the day when even the Captain's story finally ended. He dashed at the back door and threw that open, too, noticing that it had already been unlocked. Then he turned all the oven knobs to off and shut the catch on the cylinder. All too late, too, too late. Nora, in her dressing gown, her eyes wide open, lay on the cement floor, her face turned towards the day, her hands, one along her side, the other lying gently across her breasts.

The Captain fell on his knees beside her, calling: 'Nora, Nora, Nora, oh my small, lovely Nora, Nora, Nora, Nora', and he caught her up in his arms and pressed her head against his chest. Then he held her from him and was hurt and frightened by her eyes, those grey eyes, wide open, unfocused as glass, staring. He tried to lift her bodily from the cement floor. Oh but she was heavy, heavy with the unsupportable weight of her death. He laid her down again, gently, then took her under both arms and dragged her, slowly, away from the black mouth of the oven with its foul breath, in through the scullery door towards the sofa. That sound, the small but dreadfully heavy body with its dressing gown hush-hushing along the floor, the rub of the hard flesh of the heel, that sound would be the sound that would fling him often from the night-mares of his sleep into a sweaty, lonely wakefulness.

He laid her tenderly on the sofa, settled her head, tidied her dressing gown about her. Then he got on his knees beside her and tried to pray.

Down in her own room Patty had heard the sudden cries her father made. They broke in on her half-sleep like some vaguely remembered calls out of a past nightmare. Then there was nothing, and she wondered again if she had imagined the sounds. She lay, listening, until the silence grew unnatural; where were the breakfast sounds, her father's voice, singing, or joking? She got up, dressed and came quickly down the hallway. Her father was searching in the drawers of the kitchen cabinet, muttering to himself. There was a sickly-sweet smell thickening the air.

'What are you looking for, Dodgie?' she asked him quietly and she was frightened when he turned to her, his face grey and aged, his eyes red and staring. He pointed, trembling, to the couch.

That day Patty found a strength and courage she did not know she owned. She knew the calm determination she had once admired in her old Aunt Izabel; she knew, too, the day was accumulating suffering that would fall the more heavily on her later on. After these days had gone by.

Doctor Weir came. The body was taken to the hospital. The Captain sat on a wooden bench in the long narrow hall, while they waited.

'There must be a note somewhere, there must be,' he said.

'A note? What note?'

'Nora would never have gone and left us without some word of explanation, she must have left a note.'

Slowly Patty knew what he was saying. 'You mean – she knew

125

she was going to die? Suicide?'

The word, whispered, became a swift, small and blunt-headed moth, trapped in the long tunnel of the hospital corridor, flying frantically against door and window, against marble wall, against wooden ceiling, in its efforts to escape.

The Captain looked at her, pityingly. 'Nora took her own life, Patty, she couldn't stand it any more. I think Izabel was a ghost in her life. The depression wore her down. I wish we had never got that gas stove into the house... but it was easier for her, no ashes, no hauling, no dirt...'

'But she wasn't ...' Patty began, 'I mean, she was not in bad form. And the breakfast things, all set out and prepared, as usual. Why would she set the table for herself if she was going to take her life? It was an accident, Dodgie, maybe she wasn't aware until the gas got to her. You told me that she had a mat down on the floor under her knees as if she was just cleaning out the oven. You don't do things like that if you're going to take your life. And she would have written something. She would...'

The Captain's head had dropped forward onto his chest. His eyes had dulled, and his whole being aged, from within.

When they saw the body again Patty was hurt to notice how small her mother was, how the flesh was a purplish blue colour, how the body looked so other, how the complete absence of movement, the fingers lying perfectly still, seemed an affront, a diminution of the possibilities of life itself. And yet about her mother's face, here in the careless anonymity of walls and floor, of iron trestle bed, of sheets starched hard and white, there was a serenity that hurt her daughter even more.

They were together, then, as never before, closer to one another than they had been even on those special nights when the Captain heard her prayers before she got into bed and she had wrapped herself in the warm anticipation of one of his stories. For some time Patty's strength continued. The Captain clutched at her for support. Once, he saw Izabel's white, unseeing face peer in at him through the attic window in the deep fathoms of the night. He framed the words towards the window – 'I'm sorry' – but did not sound them.

After that he moved down from the room upstairs into Nora's room, touching her talcs, her brushes, her perfumes, gazing far into the dressing-table mirror as if, by looking hard and long, she might appear to him there, might speak to him and offer some simple explanation, some answer, some forgiveness. How he regretted never having learned how to speak his love to her, to find the words, the gestures, the smallness that he would need. Once, she passed him in the hallway, walking serenely from her bedroom to the kitchen, carrying a bunch of golden irises, wild creatures, that rode at peace in her arms. She did not notice him as he stood watching, afraid to interrupt her, afraid he might intrude.

Patty heard him, late at night, sobbing to himself in the bedroom. She too slept badly, going over and over in her mind every word, every action, of the days before Nora's death, trying to remember her moods, searching for something, anything, that would have been a hint, a signal, a warning. But there was nothing, nothing but a great blank wall.

They lay down together once, Patty and Josh, under the high dome of a summer sky. It was a bed of heather, the tiny purple sepals in full bloom, fine grass beneath and the heavens so blue she felt she could reach up and write in chalk across them. They had climbed up a narrow track, onto a cliff top, the sea booming below them, summer calls echoing from the distant beach, the dirty gulls risen so high above that they glowed with a translucent purity. They relished the loveliness of the day as if they lay luxuriating in a corner of paradise itself. Side by side, longing to, but not, touching. A chough swooped low, near them, out over the table edge of the cliff, the black feathers a sheen, the blood-red bill and the scarlet claws distinctly visible.

Silence between them filled with communication.

'Days like this,' Josh murmured, 'and you could begin to believe in everlasting life.'

Patty moved closer to him, her hand resting lightly on his chest. 'But the flesh is treacherous, Josh,' she said, 'suspect, subject to no law.'

He looked at her, surprised. She reached her face closer to his, quickly, and kissed him. Then she drew back a little, resting on her elbows, and pulled a tiny stem of heather from the earth. The cluster of purple bells was perfect.

'Listen,' she said, holding the stem close to his ear, touching him, 'can you hear them ringing?'

He laughed with pleasure, gently holding her wrist in his. He was shy of her suddenly. 'I think I love you, Patty,' he said quietly, the words startling them both.

Patty remained still. Her hand held the heather stem. Above them the chough exulted in the air, swooping, pirouetting, an acrobat, the world his audience, the sky his tent.

She turned and sat up then, folding her hands about her knees. She gazed away over the ocean, past the islands visible as delicate blue shapes on the horizon. As if a breath of wind could lift them like feathers, and float them into new worlds. A breeze, caressing, questioning, barely touched her face.

'I'm sorry,' Josh said.

'No, no, Josh,' she said, still watching across into space. 'It's just – it scares me, a little. I get scared easily. I think I love you too, but I'm frightened ...'

He sat up quickly, beside her, his left arm reaching and drawing her to him.

'Sometimes,' she said, her eyes closed, 'sometimes I hear voices, faint echoing sounds as if my mind were a great cave and the echo came from some ledge or fissure far within.'

He looked at her, her eyelashes were trembling, she looked so frail, a small bird on a cliff ledge, being urged towards flight.

'It began years and years ago, animal sounds, like a calling, the sound dogs make from very far away, that mournful, lonesome sound. I heard it at night, first, almost as if in a dream.'

'We all hear things, Patty, sometimes, out of dreams, out of our memories ... ' It was weak, faced with the heavy leaning of her body against him.

'This is different, Josh, it was the time of all those scares about sheep – and Izabel – that time. Then it stopped, after Izabel – as if she had taken it away with her. There was peace for a long time, together with the sorrow over Izabel's going, and the world seemed to shine, even Dodgie was other and Mamsa seemed to have found relief. Then it started all over again, the same, a far, far calling, and the pains with it, the headaches . . . '

Slowly they rocked together, slowly, slowly, and he could find no words.

She drew back from him then and held her right hand toward him. 'Look!' She said it quietly, she had grown so used to it. Her hand was distorted, the knuckles white and blue against the flesh, the fingers had become twisted, distended.

Again he could find no words. She smiled at him, and he was surprised at the strength in her eyes.

'I sometimes think I'm going to die, Josh, like my mother.'

'But you wouldn't . . . '

'I know people think that she took her own life. I don't believe she did, Josh. Dodgie has yielded to the pain of that thought. But I don't think she did – and I am pretty sure I won't, I'd be afraid to, scared stiff.' She laughed, a small, rueful laugh. 'Anyway, I won't have to.'

He was looking at her hand, it seemed to twitch and shiver. 'Has it been that way long? I mean, today?'

'Yes. Ever since you picked me up. Before that too, often, and last night.'

'Is it very painful, your hand?'

'It is, Josh. I want you to know, I have an illness, SLE, it's a form of rheumatoid arthritis, *lupus* they call it, *systemic lupus erythematosus*. *Lupus* means wolf, Josh, wolf! They are afraid, *I* am afraid, a scar will come, a scar that covers the nose, around the mouth and cheeks and it makes you look like a wolf. Josh, I get terribly scared sometimes that I will begin to look like a wolf, that I will become a wolf – they have me back on tablets, they work well, most of the time, but . . . '

She paused, then held both of his hands in hers.

'Which is why,' she said earnestly, 'I'm not going to go out with you again, Josh. Today, on a lovely day like this, the decision can be made and it will be a real one. It's not fair, on you, or on me. I'm very fond of you, Josh, and I don't want . . . I don't want either of us to be hurt . . . '

He protested, he drew her close to him, he kissed her, but she had withdrawn from him slightly, but definitely, and in spite of his continuing protestations he was relieved.

For a long time Casimir Conlon did not know what to do with his life. His voice had shrunk in confidence till it was little more than a small shout. He kept the cowpat brown door down the short hallway wide open, the window inside open too, in the hope that every possible and impossible presence might escape, to allow his own mind to dwell on vacuity. But he was like a man who had leant his shoulder so long against a wall that now that the wall had been taken away he felt as if he were forever falling sideways into nothingness. His big hands became bigger and the big hole in his life remained empty.

One day, long after Pee-Wee had taken her rightful place among the dead, Casimir Conlon decided he must take a grip on life and hope again. He would hang his butcher's apron, deliberately, where it would fit, and it would fit, he decided, on the rich-bodied shape of Vanessa O'Mahony. Vanessa came to buy chops that day and Casimir's life came up firmly against a high, gleaming wall. He stood, mouth open, eyes open, the cowpat brown door open, the buzzing of a bluebottle distinctly loud in the morning silence.

'Can I have four good loin chops, Mr Conlon? Please?'

'Chops?'

'Yes, please. Four. Four loin chops.'

'Loin chops?'

'Please.'

He turned to the table behind him. Then he turned back again, quickly. She was still there, still standing in his shop. Just across the squat lump of his butcher's block. He glanced once towards the cowpat brown door.

'You must be ... ?' he asked.

She was tall, full-breasted, wide-hipped, a pink blouse mistily outlining her breasts, denim jeans making obvious the power and beauty of her body. Casimir's eyes! The bottom of her blouse was folded up and tied in a knot, exposing her midriff, honey-coloured, the sphincter-delicacy of her navel a wonder above the big silver buckle of her belt.

'Yes,' she replied, grinning. 'That's me all right.'

'Em, Mrs O'Mahony's little one. I mean, what's this her name was. Jennifer, or Nancy, or Veronica? Something, anyway.'

'Something, I think it must have been something all right. It may well have been Vanessa, Mr Conlon. In fact, it *was* Vanessa, come to think of it. And, strangely enough, it still is. Vanessa. That's me, at least I think so. Vanessa O'Mahony.'

Honey hair, too. Warm, liquid voice. Oh Casimir's eyes!

'Vanessa, that's right. That's the name. Vanessa.'

He turned back to his table.

'A pound of – what was it again?'

'Four loin chops, if you please, Casimir.'

The name, *his* name, in her mouth, caught him a blow on the back of his neck that almost made him keel over. Her tongue around his name made it sound so strange, so exotic, so – sexy. He began to work. Chopping. Cleaning. Trimming. He turned again. She was still there. More beautiful than ever. From beyond the cowpat brown door he heard the old whining voice, 'She's not your sort, boy! You great goat, her kind's far beyant the likes of you!'

'What?' he muttered foolishly, staring into the young woman's face.

'Mr Conlon.' She spoke slowly, with a weighted seriousness. 'I was very sorry to hear of your mother's death. Very, very sorry.'

Had she heard that whining voice just now, too?

Casimir had never learned to cope with sympathy. What to say. How to accept and react. His hands waved vaguely in the air, as if to swat away the words he could not deal with. Her honey tummy. The way those lovely lips parted to reveal her teeth, perfect white teeth. He threw the chops on the weighing scales. He rubbed his hands up and down on his apron.

'The house is mine now,' he whispered in his shouting voice. 'And only myself in it. And the size of it. Are you still away in school?'

'Yes. I'm in Dublin. Computer analysis. Not "school" exactly. In university.'

He wrapped the chops in brown paper. He opened a drawer in the table and put the money she gave him into a cardboard box. He counted out her change.

'Computers,' he said, definitively.

'Computers, Mr Conlon. You could do with one in here.'

I could do with yourself in here, he thought. But perhaps the words came shouting from his eyes as he watched her. She smiled at him. Then she turned and walked slowly out of his shop. He watched the weight and firmness of her lovely arse as she left him stranded on the dry shore of his shop. He imagined his hands hefting those buttocks, knowing them, fondling ... 'Va-nes-sa,' he whispered and the sound was an exotic butterfly shimmering down that short hallway, in through the cowpat brown door and out the open window, zzziiiippppp! Surely, here he could hope to hang his apron. Casimir was scarcely fifty-two. Comfortable. A propertied man, king of his castle. Vanessa was twenty-one or so. She could be taught, brought along, cajoled. 'Va-nes-sa.'

'What was that you said, Casimir?'

The big man jumped. Maggie Muttons O'Driscoll was standing at his counter. He had not even sensed her coming in.

'Maggie! You gave me an almighty frekkin' stealin' in like that on top of me. That was Vanessa O'Mahony, that was, Mrs O'Mahony's young wan. Jaysus but hasn't she turned out a fine young woman.'

'Mrs O'Mahony's not too well, I'm told, Casimir. And that young wan up to no good while her poor mother's on her sick bed. From what I've heard.'

'What would you mean by that now, Maggie?'

'Oh you can never know with the young wans nowadays, Casimir. All sorts of notions. Up in Dublin studying, I'll be bound. Physics or chemistry or engineering or some such. I'll be bound!'

'Computers,' Casimir corrected. Proudly.

'Or some such. Not much use in this part of the world, Casimir. Not much use for physics and chemistry in your line of business, now, I'd say.'

'Computers!'

'Computers. Sure what would you be doing with a computer, Casimir?'

Casimir's grin was lewd. 'Not a lot, Maggie, not a lot. But I'd know what I could be doin' with a fine lump of flesh – if you'll pardon the expression – like that one there now!'

Maggie was startled. She stood back a moment from the counter. She gazed quickly out the door. The day was turning misty. A dreary, wet day it would be, before it closed away. She glanced towards the cowpat brown door.

'So that's the way of it, is it, Casimir?' she said, in a tone of voice that suggested she had perused all the various files and subtexts of Casimir's honest face. And come to a conclusion. An important conclusion. 'Cutlets, Casimir, please. A nice piece of neck. Neck, indeed. And chops.'

Casimir chuckled and turned towards his table.

The day was beautiful. Joshua exulted in his youth, in the firmness and strength of his body, his jumper tied easily about his waist, the neck of his shirt open, the sleeves rolled up. As he climbed he thought how easy it would be to shake off all thought of trouble or pressure in the great spaces of the mountainside. He climbed quickly, turning often to watch the island stretch itself out always more beautifully at his feet. Like a great wild cat luxuriating, he thought. Only once, when he paused to look back, did he imagine he had heard a sound, like a low, long growl, from somewhere far above him. He turned quickly, momentarily frightened and un-sure. He could see nothing. He assumed it was merely a wave breaking in the distant sea that he had heard. Above him the moorland stretched emptily away, a purple-brown glow upon it from the warmth of the day. He climbed on. Excitement held his belly.

When he topped the first ridge a shallow, damp valley lay be-tween him and the next low ridge. There was a sickly smell upon the air. He looked for the rotting carcass of a sheep but he could find nothing. The odour lingered. He picked his way cautiously across the valley; the ground was wet, soft and treacherous. How easy it would be to slip and fall into the wet earth. Somewhere, in one of these peaty holes, a carcass must lie in putrefaction. He shuddered as the smell seemed to grow stronger, all-pervasive through the warm, still air.

Then he was climbing again, up the further ridge, and the gentle sound of the sea came to him. He was sweating and growing tired. The smell grew more nauseating as he climbed. As he neared the top of the final ridge, with the smell of putrefaction forcing him to hold his left hand tightly over his nostrils, he thought he heard a low voice call his name. Once. Lingeringly. He stopped. He was startled. He waited, listening, glancing down across the low valley and around all the slopes about him.

For a long moment he was sure that Patty O'Higgins must be somewhere near him, spying on him, aware of what he was doing and of where he was heading. A great pang of guilt hurt him quickly. There was no sign of any movement, not even the stir of the couch grass under a mountain breeze. The smell seemed to have died away. He shook himself, feeling suddenly foolish.

'Patty, up here?' He whispered the words out loud, though to himself. 'Impossible. She wouldn't be able to climb this far.' And he mocked himself, the hero, scared of his own imaginings.

He topped the ridge. The air now was fresh and beautiful. Below him, across a long, sloping stretch of mountain, was the sea, breaking gently on Annagh Strand. He almost called out with the breathtaking beauty below him, the golden sand almost hidden in a cleft beneath the cliffs, the white ever-changing lines of the surf, the green sea stretching out toward the dark blue of the ocean, the silence up here, the warmth, the peace.

He was almost at the top of the low cliffs that looked over Annagh Strand when he saw someone swimming out among the waves. He lay down on his belly and looked over the cliff top. Below him on the sand he saw a small, neat heap of clothes. The figure in the sea was swimming vigorously, then turned and began to swim back in toward the strand. When she stood up in the shallow water, he could see she was naked.

The young woman came back to her neat pile of clothes. She towelled herself a little, sometimes gazing up the slopes of the cliffs, sometimes turning to watch out over the sea. Then she stretched her naked body out under the sun. Josh crawled back from the edge of the cliff and stood up. He began the climb down, his mind still disturbed, his conscience whole. As he came down towards the sand he looked towards her. She was sitting up, her hands holding her weight behind her, watching him.

'Hi, Josh,' she called and he thrilled at the sound after the lonely emptiness of his climb. 'I thought you'd never get here.'

Cyril Thornton O'Higgins spent the long, bright afternoon in an armchair before the TV set. He pulled the curtains almost closed and lit a small red lamp behind the set. There was an old black-and-white film on television and he watched it with diminishing attention. Very soon his head began to droop.

He had grown old. His hair was white now with streaks that were a pale yellow colour. His face was lined as if, indeed, he had spent years facing into the ocean storms. But his skin had remained pale and his hands had begun to shake as if already the tug of late autumn gravity was in his bones.

When he woke again, startled, Patty was sitting in another chair, watching him with that gaze of intense scrutiny and waiting he knew so well. Her head trembled slightly, her hands held the arms of her chair and her mouth was slightly open. He shook himself alert and sat up. The television had been switched off.

'Mamsa used to sit in here in the dark,' she said.

He said nothing.

'Can I open the curtains?'

He nodded. He was indifferent. The rains had begun already and were drawing their own patterns down the panes and fitfully erasing them. She stood looking out for a while.

'I will never understand why she took her own life.' His voice had lost all its vibrancy and lift. 'I loved her.'

Patty sat down again opposite him. They had had this conversation before. Many, many times.

'We don't know that she took her life, Dodgie.' She tried, once again. 'You don't set the table – oh we've been over and over this before. She suffered a great deal, you know. Her death released her from suffering.'

He was silent. Then he sighed heavily. 'Since she left me I've only half a soul,' he said.

Oh yes she knew that, knew how love can be unnerved at its own intensity, how it can be manifested in the greatest clumsiness.

'If I could have taken her suffering on myself, I'd have done so, willingly, gladly,' he added. 'And I'd take on your burden, too, Patty.'

'I know that, Dodgie, I know that.'

'Why has all this affliction stricken us? What have I done to deserve such pain?' He was near to tears now. She had seldom seen his tears but she knew, in the silence of his own room . . .

'You sound like Job on his dung heap, Dodgie.'

He would have laughed at that before, he would have marvelled at her own quiet patience before the mystery.

'Anyway,' she went on, 'pain is unimportant, it's an insect bite on the surface of the skin. It does no real harm. Mamsa's pain was worse, it was like someone else had taken hold of her and held on so that her soul couldn't breathe. You could do nothing about it, Dodgie, nobody could have done anything more.'

'You wouldn't do what she did, would you, Patty?'

'No, Dodgie, no.'

'I wish they could find the cause of your pain,' he said, 'and take it out, once and for all, like a bug they could locate and trap and take out, put it up on the table and clobber it with a great mallet. It's just,' he went on, 'when you and Mamsa suffer so much, I know it's impossible to think straight. Thinking and peace just fly away from pain, like an old cat that will leap at the barking of a dog. Pain won't allow you to think straight. Maybe that's what happened Nora. Maybe – Izabel, you know I sometimes wonder, too, about poor old Izabel.'

Patty was silent about her secret. 'Poor Izabel. Poor Mamsa. They're both on the far side of affliction now, Dodgie. It's over for them now. Poor Mamsa could only sit in the darkness and wait. Go deep down inside herself, I think that's what she used to do, and try and find some sort of quietness. And perhaps at times she found peace deep down in the dungeon of herself. But I know she never stopped loving you, Dodgie, and me, too. I know it.'

'If you could believe God was in it, it would be easier to bear. The martyrs, walking into the jaws of the lions, singing. That's choice, Patty, that's free will. But where did Mamsa's affliction come from, or yours? I cannot understand.'

'God is love, Dodgie, you have to believe that. You have to. Or how could we possibly stay alive, any of us? And love is something we cannot understand, either. You knew love, with Mamsa, and it was good. And it was difficult for you, everybody knew that. And you were good to her, and she loved you. What else is there in life? You have loved, Dodgie, and you must be grateful for that.'

He was watching her. She seemed exhausted by what she had said, as if she had spent great physical energy in bringing out the words.

'And you, Patty? How is it with you and love?'

She was looking towards him and he noticed again the slight tremor that seemed to hold her body in perpetual movement. Now all at once a different pain was in her eyes.

'I told Josh he had to find someone else, someone strong and healthy. He's good, Dodgie, Josh is a good person.'

There was a long silence between them. The rain was hitting the window outside with violence. The room had darkened.

'Sometimes, Dodgie, I feel my own mind begin to give, the sounds I hear, the things I dream, the things I imagine. And that frightens me. It's probably all these tablets, I know, but when I stop them, the pain gets worse. Intolerable sometimes now.'

She looked at him through the gloom, watching his hands worry one another. 'I've asked Doctor Weir to get me into the hospital, Dodgie, to get them to do something before I lose my mind. Before I drive you crazy with my complaining.'

He said nothing. He rose slowly from his armchair; he was an old man, slowed and stooping, weary. He reached for her and drew her up to him and embraced her, holding her small, trembling body against his. Outside the rain continued its script along the window but he could not see it through the tears that were blinding him all over again.

9

The hand reached and touched her, softly, on the shoulder. Though she was waiting for it she was startled and jumped up with a small, hurt cry. He saw a woman aged beyond her years, dressed in a red plastic coat, a red plastic hood over her head. For a time he watched her, disturbed. She watched him, too, her whole body shrinking before him, her mind trying to accept the fact that now, again, she was taken.

He spoke her name, with a kindness and gentleness that was warmth to her, she knew him at once, the relief flooding her body made her limp and she fell forward, grasping for him.

'Patty? It's you, Patty O'Higgins? Is it you?'

'Yes, Pat, yes, it's me. Pat Larry Dineen, am I glad to see you!'

He filled and overflowed the seat of his cab in the big van. Beside him she looked like a pale, small rag doll. She had taken off the red plastic rain jacket; the blouse she wore, the jeans, looked so small, but then – she was small, too, small as a child. Pat glanced cautiously at her. The van was moving slowly on towards the west. She was trembling but her face, in spite of its whiteness, looked intent, even aglow, like alabaster. She stared straight ahead. There was a smile hovering somewhere behind her lips. Her hands shivered slightly on her lap.

'So. You're going home then, Patty?'

'Yes. Home.' She smiled over at him. A weak smile that touched him greatly.

'I'm glad. The Captain will be delighted. Is he expecting you?'

'No. Poor Dodgie. I want this to be a surprise. Promise me, Pat' – and her big eyes were fixed on him – 'promise me you'll tell nobody.'

He glanced at her again. She was vulnerable, but determined.

'I'll bring you as far as the gate, then,' he said, 'and I'll leave you to surprise him yourself.' He hesitated. 'You have no suitcase or anything? From the hospital, I mean?'

'No, Pat. It wasn't a holiday I was on. No luggage. No souvenirs.' She touched his arm. 'Only memories. Here, in my head.'

He chuckled. He relished the gentle intimacy of the touch. 'My own poor head is an attic piled high with junk, Patty,' he said. 'I know what you mean.'

She was silent for a while. The road ahead unrolled itself dreamily under the van. It was a long, grey carpet. Bringing her home. She was in flight above it. The engine fumes were vaguely distressing to her but she didn't mind. She felt tired. Warm. Comforted by the big caring presence beside her.

Pat Larry was chuckling again. 'You know,' he said, 'I drove you in a van along this road before. This very road. First sight you ever got of this world was the inside of Dineen's van. Back the road a ways. Under the eye of Croagh Patrick. I remember it well. Wasn't I the very first, after your mother, after poor Nora, to welcome you into this world?'

'Mamsa told me, Pat, you were very kind. But that was someone else, Pat, that wasn't me. Not me. Not me.'

He looked across at her again. Her eyes were lightly closed. Then she looked up at him quickly and touched his arm again.

'We change, Pat, we change. We go through so much, and still, somewhere deep down inside, we remain like children, innocent, awed, uncomprehending.'

Pat nodded his head, gravely, vigorously. 'I know,' he said, 'I know exactly what you mean.'

She pressed his arm, lightly. 'And you, Pat Larry Dineen? How are things with you?'

10

The Atlantic Bar was full. Bill Cassidy, chemist, his mouth turned down in a lugubrious scowl, stood leaning against the wall, a double gin, neat, in his hand. He always stood now, in company, not certain he could rise, if he sat down, with any dignity. He was remembering with affection his hunting days in the company of Don Nealon and telling them of the day the wild goat had rushed past them in its panic.

'I heard the sound first, I don't know if Don ever heard it. A howl it was, long and bloodcurdling, like a soul in agony. Coming from somewhere high up on the cliff face, far as I could judge. I was petrified, I admit it. Don, too, Lord rest his soul. We heard it again, I did at any rate, but we never saw anything. Then this beauty of a wild goat came thundering straight at us like as if to fling us off the shoulder of the mountain. Gave us both the fright of our lives.'

'Wild dogs!' murmured Pat Larry Dineen from his corner where he sat, hunched in on himself, big as ever in his body, tired, too, from the long struggle. 'Wild dogs, that's what they keep sayin'. But Cripes, how could they open the door of my van? They opened it, the way only a hand could open it, a high handle it was on that old Ford, I had to reach up to it myself, not broken neither, opened I tell you, opened. There's no wild dog goin' as ever histed itself up seven feet and opened a fuckin' door!' and he thumped his pint of Guinness down on the yellow formica of the table in front of him.

The snug in the Atlantic Bar was warming in a dense fog of smoke, alcohol fumes and body sweat. The light, an old-fashioned bulb in an old-fashioned shade, offered its pall of yellow. There was silence after Pat's outburst. Each man looked deep into himself and put a name on the horror he had known. The Captain, morose and silent, drinking heavily, wondered when someone would say the name of Izabel. He kept his mind off Nora, that poor body slumped on the scullery floor in the only peace that she could find. He kept his mind off Patty, too, there was important business to be done, here and now, on the floor of the Atlantic Bar.

'Whipped the head off me dog an' all,' offered the usually taciturn Bomber Tuite, his great brown fist dwarfing his black pint, his words slow and ponderous as his own body. 'Th'other day an' all! Jusht up on the ridge, the mutt takes off afther this shmell. This shtink it was, everywhere it was, sicken you it would. Off she went like a bluebottle after shite. Disappeared an' all, till I seen her, down the shlope beyond, her head ripped off of her like you'd chop the head off a hen. Jaysus but I got the fuck outa' there, I can tell you. An' I'm not goin' back an' all! Sheep or no sheep. Not till all this shtuff is made simple an' open an' all and I get some answers to what's troublin' us!'

'Begun again, then, has it?' from another voice.

'Begun!' said Cassidy. 'If you asked me it never stopped, sure there's hardly a sheep to be found on the mountain these weeks past. It all began around the war, if ye remember?'

The Captain took a great gulp of his whiskey. Harder and harder it became to find any warmth or laughter now in its golden depths. His mind flickered onto Patty for a moment, and leapt away again, scorched. He said nothing, allowing the silence to spread around them, like water.

'Werewolves!'

The word was dropped loudly into the dark pool of the snug. Doctor Weir, his face pink and smooth and still baby-like, his clothes neat as always, took enjoyment these later years in the flaccid company of the Atlantic Bar. It helped him to slow down the days that seemed now to be racing towards the awful chasm.

'Canon Crowe and myself climbed up there one day, way back. Years and years ago. We saw nothing, heard nothing. But we knew there was something there. Something evil. Everywhere about us. As if each particle of air contained a piece of it. Werewolf, I remember thinking the word to myself at the time and cursing myself for a fool. I have never said the word aloud until now. Now maybe it's the time.'

There was a long silence, each hand holding firmly to its glass, each mind taking hold of the word. Then –

'Francis, Saint Francis is your man.' This sudden offering came from Godfrey Hannon, a small man who seemed to have lived all his life in a bog brown pinstripe suit and waistcoat, who sat on a high stool at the corner of the snug, his peaked cap raised quizzically on his head, and who never spoke but watched, like a god, serenely from his chosen pedestal. Every evening he came punctually at nine thirty to the Atlantic Bar, ordered a glass of stout and took his half-hour to drink it. Then he rose, pushed his stool in under the bar top, went out the back to the toilet, and left, tipping his cap to Tony on the way out.

'I remind me,' Godfrey went on, 'of Canon Crowe sayin' once all about Saint Francis of Assisi. And how the people in some town there had a wolf that come and kill hens and ducks and geese, and people too, if I recall correct – a town called – something or another, something foreign.'

'Gubbio?' offered the doctor.

Godfrey seemed offended and likely to return to his glass of stout.

'Gubbio, I say, Godfrey, that was the name of the little town. You're correct. Gubbio. The wolf of Gubbio.'

'You might be right, doctor, you might be right.' Godfrey was mollified. 'Anyways, the canon said that the saint axed them to be nice to the wolf, to feed him and all to that, to take care of him, like a pet, and they done that, and he stopped his killin'. There you have it. Now,' and he turned back to gaze into his glass.

'By God, Godfrey,' the chemist said, 'that was a fair burst of a speech.'

There was a long, ruminative silence. Tony, delivering drinks, a rag over one arm, his bald pate a contrast to his hairy chest, lost patience with the men in his snug.

'That's all a heap of shite you're after sayin', if you ask me. A heap of wet, lukewarm, stinkin' cow shite. How are youze goin' to get the sheep back on them mountain slopes, now that's what youze have got to figure out?'

'Well,' the doctor offered. 'Let me put it more plainly. It's my belief that there's some wild creature in the mountains that has got to be got rid of. Now that seems to me to be a fact. There's a killer up there. Of sheep. Cattle. Now – we've no name to put on this creature so we don't know what enemy we're facing. Without knowing what our enemy is leaves us at a loss. Right? I'm simply putting a name on this beast. And the name I'm giving it is *werewolf*.'

'Jaysus!'

'Are we back in the age of witches? Is this the middle ages? Or are we in the twentieth century? You'll have Canon Crowe up here next, performin' his rites of exorcism.' Tony's anger was palpable in the small spaces of the snug. 'Right' – Tony had slapped his wet rag off the surface of a table – 'what we have to do is to set out, all of us, all together, along the mountain, flush out this beast and kill it.'

'Now you're talkin'!'

There was a general rush of agreement.

'We'll bring weapons, anyone with a rifle, anything. And fire.'

'I have a gun,' the Captain announced suddenly. 'That rifle I captured from the Germans. And Tony, you have a bullet, a silver bullet. Remember? It's what the doctor needs for his werewolf. Shoot the bugger with a silver bullet. A German silver bullet.'

'And we must burn the cover off the mountain as we pass.' Even the old chemist was enthusiastic. 'Set fire to the heathers and ferns and flush this creature out for once and for all.'

In the wise foolhardiness of their drinking, they had named and pinpointed their prey. They drank some more, gaining courage and resolve. They set a date. They sat up more proudly on their stools. And much later they walked home through the night, their hearts and minds on fire.

Pat Larry Dineen sat in the dimness of his house. He had grown heavier with every passing year, and his loneliness had increased in proportion. Nellie the Gate O'Hara, who had helped him with the goods in his store, had withered away into the small fuchsia-wild graveyard where robins and thrushes sang and wrens darted among bramble bushes. Pat leant his right elbow more heavily out the window of his van and sank more despondently into the chairs he occupied.

He had parked the van for tomorrow's deliveries. He had done so, wearily, for the umpteenth time, without interest. The wreck of his first van was at pasture in the small field behind the house. It leant gently towards the hedge as if nodding away into sleep and the winds blew through its hollow spaces. The steering wheel was intact though the doors were gone, stopping gaps in hedges here and there about the island. The tyres Pat Larry had given away to children who came gathering material for their bonfire night. The world would swallow back Pat Larry's van, ending with the fading sign on the once high, once proud, forehead: HERE COMES DINEEN – HE DELIVERS.

Now he sat, gazing out through the open door of his shop, onto the darkness that came creeping like a cat over the mountain, down across the fields and crept, belly-flat, across the empty road, in his door, into his heart. What was the point loading his van with tins of fruit and packet soups, biscuits, flour, things to be consumed, replaced, consumed again, replaced, making the pounds that kept him tolerably well-off, well-fed, active. Round after round, up salt lanes, down again, offering chit-chat here, chit-chat there, pausing, turning up another lane ...

Even now the spry and lovely Maud Tuohy came into his mind the way a porpoise comes gambolling suddenly into the bay, the way a seal will poke its head out of the current, silently, and watch towards the land. Maud, grown buxom, large-hipped, soft-fleshed. Maud, whom he spied on as she cycled past, her skirt blown up over her thighs; and at times her buttocks moving languorously inside her jeans, her bright face cheery as a meadow filled with buttercups when he greeted her. He would call to her, a catch taking him in the throat, making him gulp his words, making him conscious of his bulky awkwardness against her beauty until wild Eamonn Darby, back from years in Birmingham, swept her away and married her, scything through Pat Larry's meadow of bright flowers with terrifying and irreversible rapidity.

Maud Darby. Never sounded right on anybody's lips, according to Pat Larry Dineen. Quickly she had fallen into flesh, so quickly the children came and Maud never cycled past his door again. Oh yes, he delivered, up the rough sandy lane to her door, his heart pounding as he drew nearer, his mind growing into hurt as he watched her rapid decline, Eamonn Darby spending evening after evening in the pub, avoiding child and home and small farm until Pat Larry dropped away into silence, his soul aching.

Now he thought he heard a soft shuffling sound from the dark outside. He waited. Listening. Gradually he grew aware of a foetid stench heavy on the air. Again he was sure he heard a sound somewhere around the angles of the house. He stood up, quietly, reached for the slash-hook he kept ready behind the door. Pat was not afraid, why should he be? What was there left to lose? He edged to the doorway and peered into the deepening darkness. He could see the outline of the back of his van, he could hear the soft breathing of the wind in the fuchsia hedge.

He waited. He could hear no other sounds. The stench remained on the air, vaguely reminding him of the stench left long after a lorry filled with hacked shark flesh had gone by. But this was something subtler than that, a sickening smell yet mingled with something sweet, vaguely seductive, charged with an ingratiating musk. He stood, still as the stump of a tree, the blade held firmly in his hand, prepared.

He stood a long time. The smell lingered on the air, fading slowly. He heard no further sounds. He sensed the rise and fall of his own body with each slow breath. Softly a deep sadness settled back on his life. Only the sickly-sweet insinuation of the smell remained. The slash-hook fell from his hands and clattered with an ugly, alarming sound on the concrete floor. Pat was shaken by a great surge of anger and resentment. He bunched his fists and struck them against the jamb of the door. A cry of rage came to the surface of his chest and he held it down with difficulty.

Then he stepped out into the night and slammed shut the door of the house behind him. He climbed into the cab of his van and reversed out onto the road. The van roared in protest as he pressed the accelerator to the floor in a rush of blinding anger and started out with a shower of stones he knew not where. He drove blindly for a time, using no lights, driving the van like a murdering hulk through the near darkness. He had often joked that he could drive every road of the island blindfolded.

He stopped the van abruptly at the end of Maud Darby's lane. He could see a light from the Darby house. Maud would be at home. The children would be in bed. No doubt Eamonn would be in the pub, lording it. She would be vulnerable. Perhaps willing. Surely understanding.

Pat climbed down out of the cab of the van and walked quickly and quietly over the sandy ground. As yet he had no clear idea of intent. The crude limbs of furze bushes stuck up into the night about him. His feet made a whisperful, crunching sound on the lane. Far away a dog was barking fitfully, like an echo, as if vaguely aware of some threat along the night. The sky was vast above him, clouds drifting westwards, a few stars brilliant in their distance and mystery. A clutch of sorrow took Pat Larry in the throat. He stumbled, hesitated, then strode on. What was there to lose? If he could snatch even a moment of ecstasy, of knowledge, of love?

He lifted the iron latch on the small front gate. He felt astonishment that the low bungalow before him was not somehow loud in alarm. He knew there were flowers growing in little patches of soil on either side of the path. Flowers she had planted and tended. How grateful Pat would have been for such flowers. How he would have sat with her, on quiet evenings, listening to her, sharing his life with her, sharing hers. She should have known, he thought, suddenly bitter against her, she should have known his need, his longing. She should have seen his goodness, his kind and generous heart, how he would have cared for her, taken all her dreams and fulfilled them, taken her life and put it

147

before his own, loving her, watchful, tender, she ought to have been aware.

He went softly along the front of the house, towards the window. A beam of yellow light was falling across the tiny lawn, cutting at a sharp angle towards a hedge. The curtains were drawn, leaving a parting of several inches. Cautiously Pat peered into the light of another life. Maud was there, his own Maud Tuohy, her profile to the window, sitting on a high-backed chair, upright, still, as if she were waiting. Everywhere about there was silence. She should have known, Pat thought, and perhaps she did know, and it was not yet too late. Perhaps . . .

He turned back abruptly towards the door. An overwhelming wave of emotion was taking him, a mixture of anger and sorrow and loss, of despair and hope, an overwhelming sense of longing, physical, emotional. His body trembled. His eyes blinked rapidly in spite of himself. He must have sobbed, or else his foot had stumbled against a stone for suddenly the door was opened and he was caught, cowering like a hare, in the net of light from within. Maud Tuohy, beautiful as ever, stood before him.

'Eamonn?'

She called the name tentatively, and it struck Pat a blow in the chest that made him gasp.

'Pat? Pat Larry? Is that you?' Her voice, so soft, so considerate, so welcoming.

'Maud, I . . . I . . . ' he stumbled, helpless, lost.

'Is there something wrong, Pat? Has something happened? Is Eamonn all right?'

Eamonn! Fuck Eamonn! How can you give a moment's care for that bastard who doesn't care for you? *I* care, Maud, *I* care. I have always cared, I love you, Maud, Maud, Maud, I need you, I want to fall onto the earth with you, before you, under you, I want you to walk on me, Maud, to use my body as your ground, to shelter your loveliness from the wet earth, I want to take your weight on mine, my lovely Maud, so that you can rest in me and then I will know my worth and I can begin to find rest in you. Maud. Maud.

'No, Maud, no. Nothing's happened. Everything's all right.'

'Then what, Pat, what? It's late. Are you all right? Will you come in?'

Yes, oh yes, Maud, yes, I'll come in, and you will stretch your arms wide and embrace me, and then you'll kiss me, softly, softly, softly, on the lips, like the sun touching a silver drop of rain on the scarlet tongue of the fuchsia flower and I will lift you up in my strong arms and carry you gently and lay you down gentle as a feather, Maud, as a flower of bog asphodel breathed on by the summer breeze, and I will open the buttons of your dress . . .

'Eh, no, no thanks, Maud, I just em . . . '

She stood watching him, beautiful in her womanhood, in her stillness, the way her white bare arm curved upwards to the door, the way her hair caught the light of the lamp behind her, the way her neck . . . And he, Pat Larry Dineen, Puddings, the Reek, fat, greasy, old. His life seemed to sag wholly at that moment, all rage and anger and hope falling from him as if his soul had fled him, and he stumbled, as if he would fall, collapse rather, like an emptied sack, at her feet. She gave a small short cry of distress and reached for him but he straightened quickly and gathered himself back into life. Knowing, fully and without any hesitation, that if he had anything at all left in his life, he must not destroy it, he must not damage it, he must not hurt her, above all, not Maud, not Maud Tuohy.

'I'm sorry, Maud, I heard a noise below, I was worried you were all right. Is everything all right? Are you safe?'

She looked at him for a moment, as if she did know.

'Yes, yes, thanks, Pat, yes, I've heard nothing here.'

'All right so, I'm sorry to disturb you, Maud, I'm sorry. Sorry to disturb you . . .' and he turned from her quickly, the light from the door falling over the flowers. He imagined he knew their lovely scent, of freshness, beauty, and he hurried to the gate.

'Pat,' she called after him softly into the night. Was it a call, a plea, a cry for help, or merely a vague concern?

He waved his hand quickly into the air, then he was gone, closing the gate behind him and running, stumbling, sobbing, down the lane. He did not look back, horrified in case he might see himself still standing at Maud's door, his hands rising maniacally towards her. He climbed into the van, reversed into the lane and drove quickly away. His petrol tank was full, ready for deliveries, he would drive as far as he could from Maud's door and from himself standing there, and when he was too tired to drive further he would crawl into the back of his van and fall asleep, waiting for the light of another day to waken him.

Maggie Muttons O'Driscoll, priest's housekeeper, came in to Casimir Conlon's shop. It was Saturday. The door of the slaughter-house was closed as she passed into the yard. She was glad. It was hard to relish the taste of chops after you had glimpsed the poor slaughtered creatures hanging upside down in that gloomy place, drip-dripping their blood into an enamel bath. She noticed the great lock Casimir had placed on the door. Times change, change surely, and never for the better, Maggie thought.

She was surprised to find the door to the shop closed too. It was late afternoon but Casimir had not yet sold her what she needed. She peered in through the window. He was sitting on a wooden chair, fastening the laces in great black boots. She rapped on the glass. The poor man leapt in astonishment.

'Maggie,' he said when he opened the door, 'is it only yourself that's in it?'

Casimir, for all his flesh and his florid feathers, looked paler than usual.

'Whatever is amiss, Casimir Conlon, man? Surely you're not beginning to pine after poor Pee-Wee at this late hour, God rest her soul?'

'No, Maggie, no indeed, though her very presence in the room beyant was a class of a comfort to me.'

'Of course, Casimir, of course. Sure every man, don't we all know it, and every woman too, needs the comfort of another human being always close by.'

'You never said a truer word, Maggie . . .' and the image of Vanessa, naked but for the floral apron hanging at this moment behind his kitchen door, busy at the oven and smiling over at him, floated through Casimir's head. 'You never said a truer word.' He sighed a big hopeless sigh.

'Can I get four nice chops, Casimir, for myself and the canon, or are you for taking your holidays for yourself already?'

Casimir reached for his blood-stained butcher's apron from the hanger by the fridge. 'Maggie, the heart within me is all minced up till I don't know whether I'm a sheep or a butcher. I'm after hearin' the great howlin' of the beast itself that long ago stole my carcasses. I've a lock on the slaughterhouse door but divil the bit o' good a lock'll do against the likes of that creature. Four chops is it?'

'Four of your finest and leanest, Casimir, please. And what in the name of God are you talking about? Howling and prowling indeed. It's in the church of God you should be, on your knees before the Lord and the canon, making the spirit of your poor departed mother happy with the cleansing of your soul. There now!'

'And would you like a piece of neck too, Maggie, now, to ease the burden of prayers on Sunday?'

'No mockery, Casimir Conlon, no mockery! And I see you're all dressed up, boots and all, for the big outdoors? Out courting a sweet young girl, I'll be bound?'

'Ah Maggie, sure is there one on this earth who'd have me?'

'Now Casimir Conlon, stop that sly fetching for compliments. Sure wouldn't a woman be proud to come and keep for you in this fine place; a touch of smartening here and there, a lick of paint and a spit of polish and she'd be as comfortable as a kitten in a blanket.'

'There's that young Vanessa one now, Maggie, would raise the hair on a man's back, what?'

'Is that the way it is, Casimir? Vanessa. Vanessa O'Mahony. God help us, Casimir, she's only a slip of a thing, her head filled with music and discos and drugs and her own poor mother coughing away her last moments of life. How are you on the disco scene, Casimir?'

'I never got much beyant "The Wind that Shakes the Barley", Maggie, but there was a time when I had a neat pair of legs to put under me.'

'What you need, Casimir, is a good hoult of a woman who'll cook your meals and iron your suits and keep you warm in the long winter nights, staying in beside you instead of gambolling and car-olling all over the island. And isn't the canon getting crotchety and difficult and far too keen on his drop of whiskey to appreciate the blessing a fine housekeeper can be?'

Casimir rolled the chops in brown paper and eyed Maggie

circumspectly. About his own age and shape, indeed. Comfortable, that's the word. Comfortable. He frowned to himself, turned away for a moment to get some twine. Too old for having children, and that's a blessing for a man who has walked beyant the first few turns of the road. Plenty of flesh on her a man could get his teeth into. No Vanessa, mind. Sexy wouldn't be the word. Nor erotic. Kinky, though, and he chuckled to himself; Maggie Muttons O'Driscoll, priest's housekeeper, kinky! But comfortable now, no doubt about that. A good roll in her. Like a thick-woolled ewe.

Maggie was gazing vaguely towards the door of the room beyant. Drumming her fingers on the surface of the butcher's block.

'And what about yourself, Maggie, and the discos?'

'Well, Casimir, I'd be more the one for a nice stroll of an evening, an easy chat, and my arm linked into the arm of another, or for stopping home of a wet evening, enjoying a fat apple tart with a dollop of custard on the top of it, and me and him sitting off by the open fire, or maybe watching one of them soaps on the TV with a delicate little tumbler of whiskey and warm water in my fist, a whisper of sugar in it and a smartening of cloves, slippers on my feet, and the certainty of company I knew and got along with.'

'Sounds good, Maggie. Sounds very good now. Maybe . . .'

'Yes, Casimir?'

'I'd drop you back in the van now, Maggie, except that I have to join the men on the mountain. There's a hunt on this evenin', you know, a scourin' of the mountainside for this wild goblin or hound or devil or whatever has been hauntin' our lives too long. I'll better be gettin' away with them now.'

'Did you ever hear such nonsense! I'm surprised, Casimir Conlon, surprised. And they're already burning the mountainside, I could see the smoke myself drifting away over the hills as I came down. But you were sayin', Casimir, we were sayin' . . .'

Casimir looked at her again. Her face was a kind face, her skin still amost baby-smooth, her grey eyes bright but tinged with melancholy. He would like to see that face warm up and smile at him. He would like that. She had a lot of years within her yet, a lot of comfortable years. She blushed lightly under his gaze. She looked away, out the door of the shop. And he could always let his eyes feast on the more shapely, impossible flesh of Vanessa and eat and drink her up in his own mind whenever he felt so inclined. You can always look in the shop window, he thought, without having to go in and buy.

He was holding the bundle of chops towards Maggie. She was looking into his eyes now. They were quiet for a long moment.

'Me and you, Casimir Conlon and Maggie O'Driscoll. Yes.'

From the room beyant a floorboard creaked a moment, and the silence stretched, expectant, hovering.

He said it again, feeling the sound, testing it: 'Casimir Conlon and Maggie O'Driscoll. There now!'

Maggie looked out the shop door towards the distant sea. 'Is that a proposal, Casimir Conlon?'

She surprised herself. She was trembling. Suddenly cold. One moment out of a long life. One moment imagined and dreamed of and dismissed as impossible. Come suddenly. And unexpectedly. Or was it unexpected? She could not tell. One moment. That's all. And when it passed? What would there be when the moment passed away, following all the millions of moments?

'By God, Maggie, do you know what? It is! It's a proposal!' And Casimir Conlon thumped his big fist down on his butcher's table as a great warm golden light passed over his body.

She put her hand down on his and smiled. 'Casimir, I'll go back and give the canon his dinner. Then I'll slip out and come back to you here. He'll not miss me, God help him. Let you not go on this mad caper in the mountains and we can have a little chat here together, just me and you. I'll bring down a bottle I have in the cabinet above. What about that, Casimir, now? what about that?'

'Ah God, Maggie. That'll be fine. Just fine.'

Canon Donal Crowe was driving home from the shops in town. His car, a Morris Minor, had become as much a part of him as his black biretta; there were twenty-five thousand miles up on the clock – second time around. The car, elderly and creaking, was the one true facet of his early conviction as a young priest – his devotion to poverty, to chastity, to the poor – that he had retained. Its leatherette seats were polished to a grey vagueness from use, they reeked of dignity; the wooden dashboard was dark brown but all the dials still worked. To the right and left of the car the indicators were the original yellow signals that flapped up and out, like chicken wings, when he wished to turn. Only the brakes were questionable, a problem the canon had learned to solve in his own way.

He was particularly happy today. The woods were his favourite shades, brown, yellow and ochre. The air was still and sharp and soon, he knew, the wild duck would be coming in again over the ocean, the nights would be dark, he could sit at home beside a lively fire and listen to the plays on the radio. In the boot he had his groceries, the usual necessities, and a bottle of Irish whiskey discreetly slipped in at Sweeney and Sons, General Merchants. Even Maggie would be more mellow in weather like this, and he would not feel afraid to ask for his favourite mutton stew twice a week.

As the canon came slowly round a bend on the road Doctor Weir was coming against him in his big new Austin. The doctor was going, as usual, at an unconscionable speed and the canon drew in to the left-hand side of the road, his two left wheels up on the grassy bank, not far from the edge of the drain. Doctor Weir flew by without noticing the dilemma of the poor priest, without remarking the fingers lifted in salute. And Canon Crowe was stunned to see the good doctor reading a newspaper opened out in front of him across the driving wheel. My God! Was this what it was coming to – speed, speed, speed, no time any more for the customary discretions?

Canon Crowe shook his head and tried to settle back into his peaceful reverie. Other cars overtook him, several came against him; each time he slowed down, allowing them room, giving them as much of the road as he dared. Some of them hooted in derision at his snail's pace or in annoyance or in greeting, he was incapable of determining. What he was sure of was that they were all in the greatest hurry possible to wherever and whatever they were heading to. And *he* knew what they were all heading to – death, that was what. Death. He smiled to himself. Might get there myself sooner than any of them, but at my own speed, he chuckled, at my own speed.

Just one sick call, then up the gravel drive to his house, hand over the groceries (minus one bottle) to Maggie, settle himself before the fire. He would listen to the radio, then when Maggie took away the tray and said good night he would have a whiskey or two, quieting the beast within, then think out his sermon for the morning, and dream.

Mrs O'Mahony was very ill. The canon went upstairs with the daughter, Vanessa, and went quietly into the room. (Vanessa – a bright and attractive girl, but what a name. Where on earth did they find such an artificial name? Giving the girl strange ideas, never came to Mass at all, brushed aside all the conventions wore tight jeans and a blouse tied up to display her navel. The old monsignor before him had been quite a bush-basher, flushing out the couples after dances, but nowadays they just went and kissed lasciviously in public, ran their hands every which way all over one another in full view of everyone.)

Poor Mrs O'Mahony. She was lying flat as a board and almost as still, on the bed, her eyes closed, her breathing like that of an old lorry climbing the narrow road up the mountainside. And she was yellow, shrivelled, a leaf alone on a bough, ready to fall. Into what darkness? He had given her the Last Sacrament just a few days ago, now he knelt by the bed, took one of her hands in his and prayed quietly for an easy passage for her across the great gulf and over into God's holy ground. The hand felt like tissue paper in his own; it was all he could do to hold onto it. He closed his eyes and concentrated on the name of the Lord.

Vanessa stood by, watching him. He wondered if she prayed. He passed his hands over Mrs O'Mahony in blessing, and went quietly out of the room. Vanessa came after him down the stairs.

'Poor thing,' he ventured, 'but bless her, she never did a wicked deed in her long life. She's for heaven before we even know she's dead.'

The priest eyed the young woman but Vanessa wasn't drawn. She went along the hallway while he hovered.

She turned to him. 'Would you care for a cup of tea before you go?'

Said, he thought, with a twinkle in those lovely eyes; as if she ... could she know of his penchant for whiskey? The thought hurt him, sharply.

'No, no, thank you, Vanessa, no.'

'Right,' she pronounced, dismissively. Not even a 'Father' nowadays, God help us.

'I'll just have to get home now, Vanessa, with the groceries, to Maggie, you know. But you will ring me if there's any change in your mother, won't you now?'

'Sure I will, but there's no point in dragging you out in the middle of the night, is there? You've done all you can do, and if she dies sure she'll have had all the consolation you can give her.'

'H'mmmm, well, yes, Vanessa, I suppose you're right. Still, when one of the congregation goes to her eternal reward after so many years of unstinting service, it's a consolation to ourselves to see another saint making her way to the Throne on our behalf. Her spirit will fly close to us on its way to the Heavenly City, the breath of her flight will brush against our cheeks as she goes by.'

'If that's what you want that's all right with me, I'll give you a ring, so, if that's what you mean.'

She let him out.

No sense of mystery at all in the young ones going the roads nowadays, everything had to go and be used up at once, go for it, get it, use it, throw it away. Instant coffee, instant tea, instant love, use it up and fling it away into the bin. Disposable souls. God help us. No sense of time, much less of eternity. And poor old Mrs O'Mahony will be given a workman-like funeral but they'll go through it without belief in any of it, no faith, no hope, nothing.

On the gravel driveway up to his house there was a gentle slope; this made stopping the old Morris Minor much easier for Canon Crowe; the brakes were temperamental, so he had to time things carefully to have the car come to a natural halt by itself; indeed he had often been seen leaping from the car and rushing in front of it to stop it himself, broad shoulders against the bonnet; he had two old hand irons to put in front and behind a wheel, to hold it, once it stopped. Not having gone faster than twenty-five miles an hour in his life he had never seen the need to get expensive brakes fitted to the old car. This time everything worked out perfectly, the car ghosted to a stop right outside the kitchen door. Thank God for the voluminous folds of a black soutane, he thought, as he ferried the whiskey down to his study.

That evening Canon Crowe slipped into a comfortable sleep by the fire. He had eaten well, Maggie had cleared away the things, and he had decided on a nap before getting the sermon together. The room was quiet, there was only the ticking of the clock on the mantelpiece and the gentle shiftings of the fire. He dozed.

He came to with a start. He thought he had heard a knocking at his door. He glanced at the clock: a few minutes before ten. Maggie would have gone to bed. He went to the door and looked out into the hallway. There was a dim night light burning but no sign of anyone about. He came back into the room and sat down again in the depths of his favourite chair. The lines of a poem came into his head:

> While I nodded, nearly napping, suddenly there came a tapping,
> As of someone gently rapping, rapping at my chamber door.

He chuckled. Partly because of his own name, but mostly because he loved the rhythm and sound and mystery of the poem, the canon knew all of Edgar Allen Poe's 'The Raven' by heart. When he went into the local school, and stood before Josh MacLean's little boys, he often recited parts of it for the children. He offered its beauty as a contrast to the rubbish they all watched nightly on television.

Canon Crowe poured himself a small glass of whiskey and placed it on the mantelpiece close by his chair. He set himself to thinking about his sermon for the following day. October, mid-October, no special day, just an ordinary Sunday, a 'Sunday in ordinary time', as if the whole of life wasn't ordinary anyway, nothing unusual ever occurring about here. He laughed at himself, remembering his Latin, remembering his calling. 'Sure isn't life itself a miracle,' he said, and reached for the golden liquid.

He read the lessons in the missal; from Isaiah, *The Lord will wipe away the tears from every cheek; he will take away his people's shame everywhere on earth, for the Lord has said so.* Lovely, lovely. Mrs O'Mahony's prone, sad body came before his mind, he thought of Vanessa and how much she was missing, unaware that there was a shroud over her life because she did not even begin to believe in the great mysteries. He took a big sip from his whiskey and spoke out loud:

> And the raven, never flitting still is sitting, still is sitting
> On the pallid bust of Pallas just above my chamber door;

And his eyes have all the seeming of a demon's that is dreaming
And the lamp-light o'er him streaming throws his shadow on the
   floor;
And my soul from out that shadow that lies floating on the floor
Shall be lifted – nevermore!

The canon sighed with satisfaction. Tomorrow he would give
them a good sermon; early winter, death on the trees, in the fields,
the old and weak facing into another winter . . . tell of the beauty
that lies beyond . . . face up to the invisible, turn away from material
things . . . turn towards the incorruptible, the mystery, the glory . . .
   Again he thought he heard knocking at the door; he called out
'come in, come in' but there was no response. He went to the door
and opened it; nobody. He went out to the kitchen; Maggie would
have gone to bed; he checked the front door; nobody. The wind
was rising; there were splutters of rain against the windows; it
would be a wet night. He closed the door of his room, glad of the
warm fire; he drew closer to it, took another drink and read the
Gospel for the next day.
   'The kingdom of heaven may be compared . . . son's wedding . . .
they would not come . . . oxen, fatted cattle . . . come to the wedding . . . they would not come.'
   Yes, he would tell them of the great feast prepared for them in
that lovely country just beyond their eyes, a country where Death
has been destroyed, and where every tear has been wiped away. Tell
them . . .
   The phone shrilled from the far corner of the room. He was
startled. It was Vanessa. Her soft warm voice came to him out of a
great distance.
   'Father Crowe, mother is dead. She died very peacefully just a
few minutes before ten. You asked me to tell you.'
   'God be good to her soul. I'm very sorry for your trouble now,
Vanessa. I'll come over right away.'
   Vanessa insisted there was no need for him to come. Her mother
was dead. She would lie as she was until morning. There was noth-
ing more that anyone could do tonight.
   'But I would like to say some prayers with you and your mother,
Vanessa,' he pleaded. 'I'm sure she would have wanted that.'
   'Well, we're all very tired and we want to go to bed soon. We'd

much prefer if you came sometime tomorrow, after Mass maybe, and we can discuss the arrangements.'

'Very well, then, Vanessa, it is a rather bad night, but I will go over to the church now and offer a few prayers for her soul, and for you all. God be with you this night, Vanessa. Good night now.'

'Good night, Father.' Softly, across a very great distance.

So, Mrs O'Mahony's soul had left the lower valley and had begun its flight to the house of God. Canon Crowe went back to the fire and poured himself another glass of whiskey. He would go to the church. It was only five minutes down the road; he would be back in no time; it was the very least he could do now that one of his parishioners had left for ever, left for the great banquet at the table of the King. 'Quoth the raven, nevermore!'

He sat down to write a few notes in an attempt to keep his thoughts together for tomorrow's sermon. Now he could talk of Mrs O'Mahony, bringing into the general flow of his sermon the particular example of a holy death, of a passage from this island to the island of the blest. It was ten thirty, the time between times, the time of the first deep darkness of the night. He took another drink, drained the glass, then filled it again. He felt cold and he hunched in against the fire. Tomorrow, the twenty-eighth Sunday in ordinary time; it was a long haul, this, between the mystery of Easter and the wondrous beginning of Advent; these times that hang between times are the hardest to cope with; they bring emptiness, they need to be filled with God.

The whiskey was filling his insides with pleasurable fire. He must take Vanessa on, bring her to an awareness ... She would be a wondrous fish to drown ... to *land*, on the shores of the Lord. He downed the glass of whiskey, to fortify himself ... He slopped some down his soutane and onto the chair. Oops, Maggie will be crosh. *Cross!* He chuckled to himself, poor Maggie, poor spinster Maggie, no doubt fast asleep, like any log or dog or hog ...

> Back into the chamber turning, all my soul within me burning,
> Soon again I heard a tapping somewhat louder than before.

The words went through his mind and he looked quickly towards the door. Silence. He looked around the room. Nothing. Had the spirit of Mrs O'Mahony brushed past him in its flight? He found his coat. He went out into the dark October night.

It was raining and the wind swept round the corners of the house; the gravel pathway was visible but he could find his way to the church in total darkness. As he came out the gate and over the cattle grid onto the road something seemed to catch him by the ankles and he fell. He sat on the road for a moment, feeling his knees and hands and elbows where he had fallen; he grew aware that he was a little dizzy. And he had dropped his glasses. He felt around on the wet ground until he found them. Not a good start, this, he chuckled, picking himself up. Sacerdat ... sacerdotal, that's the word, sacerdotal dignisshhy ...

He put on the light in the sacristy and went through onto the altar; it was very cold in the church; the wind outside seemed to gain a special power against the high angles of the building, rising to a howl and fading away into a series of moans and groans. The rain battered against the stained-glass windows. There was only the red sanctuary lamp in the church, and a small rectangle of yellow light falling across the altar from the open sacristy door.

Canon Crowe knelt on the lowest step and gazed up at the sanctuary light; only then did he notice that it was not rain on his glasses that refracted everything – both lenses were cracked. His heart sank. Without the glasses he could hardly see a foot in front of him. He tried to pray. He imagined himself stumbling on the altar tomorrow during Mass; but then wasn't he their canon? A little stumble here and there would only arouse the sympathy of his congregation.

There was a sudden scuffling noise in the darkness of the church behind him. He turned but could see nothing through the darkness. Then there was a rush of air somewhere in the body of the church and the priest thought he caught a glimpse of something white or grey move swiftly from one darkness to another. Then there was silence. He realised that his body had stiffened with fear; he tried to call out, but he could not. The wind seemed the louder outside and the rain the heavier.

'Darkness there and nothing more.'

He turned back to the altar but remained conscious of that great black space behind him. He spoke the words out loud, 'Our Father, who art ...' and at once a dull shushing sound came again and it was followed by a scraping noise from somewhere out in the dark- ness. The echo in the church made it difficult to locate where the noise was coming from. Canon Crowe thought of the candle-white body of Mrs O'Mahony lying on her bed of death.

'Now, dear God, oh my dear God, be with me now and in the hour of my agony,' he whispered aloud.

An answering whisper came from the space behind him but Canon Crowe knew that if it were truly a voice then it was not, not, *not* a human voice. He turned on the steps and sat, watching out through his cracked lenses onto the blackness. He promised, at once, in memory of the kind and saintly Mrs O'Mahony, that he would not touch another drop of whiskey. The sound was still there, a faint, scratching, almost whispering sound that seemed to fill the space, to be here and there and everywhere all at once.

Words came unbidden into Canon Crowe's mind and he spoke them quietly at the darkness:

Prophet, said I, thing of evil! prophet ssshhtill, if bird or devil!
Whether Tempter sent, or whether tempest tossed thee here ashore,
Desolate yet all undaunted . . . Desolate yet all – undaunted . . .

For the first time in many years Canon Crowe forgot the lines. He turned his fear and sorrow onto himself and stood up shouting: 'Fool! Criminal! Sinner! I here confess before my God and before you, you torturing spirit, that I have sinned and do repent me.'

His outburst was answered by a total silence from the space before him. For a moment he felt a cold breeze move about his head. He bowed and waited for the blow he knew must surely fall. Nothing happened. The church was as still as the inside of a coffin.

The image of Mrs O'Mahony rose again in his brain, the old matron, the widow, the saint, there she stood in her apron, her red fists raw from the washing, hair tied with a furious hatred of what a woman's hair can be, like a cock of wet hay behind her head; her face was contorted with its certainties, its virtue, its delight in woe; her mouth was moving crookedly, suggesting, criticising, cursing the terrible draw of drink that makes men mad. And Canon Crowe knew that it was she who was in the church with him, trying to destroy him for his failure to be with her as she passed out of this valley of tears. He screamed, he screamed and screamed and held his body taut into the scream, finding some relief. As the echoes died away he knew what he had to do.

He stumbled back up the altar steps and took the crucifix from its stand above the tabernacle; he went to the sanctuary light and lifted out the floating candle. Slowly and unsteadily he went down the steps and out into the body of the church, calling out: 'I rebuke thee! I rebuke thee! I abjure thee and summon thee forth from this darkness. Evil spirit, begone from this holy ground; get thee gone into the realms of evil whence thou hast come. I rebuke thee in the name of the Father. I rebuke thee in the name of the Son. I rebuke thee in the name of the Holy Ghost!'

He waited for some response but there was none, only the barracking of the winds and rains against the walls of the church. He whispered the words once more, 'I rebuke thee!'

He felt at peace then, and very, very tired. He stood quietly for a time, the small light in his hand shivering with his shivering, and he knew that it was over, that he had won, that he had gone far beyond this Saturday in ordinary time and had survived. He sat down against one of the benches, exhausted; he curled himself into himself and thanked the Lord. 'My brothers and sisters,' he said, half-aloud, 'my dear brothers and sisters, today is a wondrous day though it may seem to be no different from any other. Today, the twenty-eighth Sunday in ordinary time, I have wondrous things to tell, woundroush, wonderish shingsh ...' and the canon, worn out, slipped into a long, restoring sleep.

11

The road unrolled dreamily under her. It was a long, grey carpet. She was in flight above it. She looked over at the big man beside her in the cab. Dineen. He delivers.

He was nodding, gravely. She pressed his arm.

'And you, Pat, how is it with you?'

He found himself, quickly and fluently, telling her of his pain of the night before. Of his visit to Maud, his agony, his distress. He found himself spreading his life out before her, something he had never done before, ever, not even to the missionaries in Confession, not even to himself. Her eyes remained on him, her fingers touched his arm. It was as if her presence drew his inmost thoughts out into the bright light of day. He talked on, his soul unclenching like a flower. And the road went by, trees, bushes, villages, and the mountains of the island appeared on the horizon.

He told her he had spent the night in his van away on the coast of Mayo, at Downpatrick Head. He had walked, slowly, up the long slope. 'My mind was like – I don't know what, Patty, empty, but full of noises, like gurgling, sloshing about. And my body felt so heavy. I'm heavy, anyway, I'm the Reek, Puddings, I know that but this was different, a hopelessness. There were these blowholes, the sea coming under the cliffs, reaching far, far in, and crashing up into the air through the earth, like a fountain. I looked down into one of those holes. Not as if I was going to do anything, like throw myself in or anything, I'm not like that, I'd be terrified of it, but sort of fascinated by it, by the violence, the beauty of it, the great reach of the sea and I felt that one day the strip of hill I was standing on would all be eaten away by the sea, digested, thousands and thousands of years from now. And the thought of that gave me a bit of relief, I don't know why. And then, up on the head, there's this sea-stack, like a mighty slice of cake cut out of the earth, you can see all the layers and layers of rock, thick and thin, and the whole stack about thirty or forty feet out in the sea, on top there's grass, a small patch. I wanted to be out there, away from the world, lying on that patch of grass on top of the sea-stack, on top of those millions and millions of years, fading into the ground, fading, melting away. I don't know, Patty, something to do with how small we are, and how short a time we are on the earth, the strange hungers and angers and longings and hopelessness somewhere inside, and there I stood, the night coming down, the sea birds settling on their ledges, the waves breaking far below me, that stack standing there, and time working away, working away. I knew my own sadness didn't matter a damn, not to the world, sea or sky, not to anybody in the whole universe, and really, one day, it would not matter any more to me, either. I came down the hill, got in the van and slept peacefully. I had a hearty breakfast this morning in a café and headed home. And saw you.'

He stopped, at last, suddenly embarrassed. She had not taken her eyes from his face, nor her hand from his arm. She had nodded at times, she had understood. Yes, she had whispered, I know, I know.

She looked at him silently for a while, her head trembling slightly, her eyes intent upon him. Then she said: 'You're a very fine person, Pat Larry, a very fine person. Dodgie used to say that with most people "the deeper you'd go the shallower they'd get". Not with you, Pat Larry, not with you. You're a very fine man, and Maud Tuohy would have been lucky to have married you.'

He grinned, sheepishly, chuffed.

'And you have known what love is, Pat, you've felt it, experienced it, understood it, and it's a wonderful thing.' She pressed his arm again. 'You're a good person, Pat Larry, and I'm glad it was you that came along and found me.'

He felt strong again, sitting up in his cab, the hills ahead, his shop, his communion with himself and with the evenings. And he would have things to say, later; he would have a cause; he would have things to remember, to insist on; he would have names for love, he would be a witness. Giving his own testimony.

But for now ... She asked him to let her out as they came near the church on the island. She would pray a while. First. Then, she told him, she would go home. She would be happy to be home. Happy. Well, at last. And at peace.

He got out of the cab and came round to help her down. He lifted her under both arms and hoisted her. She rested her hands on his arms and smiled down at him. She was light as a butterfly, he thought, delicate enough to be whisked away by the slightest breeze. He set her on the ground, his heart full. He handed her down her small red plastic coat. She put it on and it seemed to be too big for her, to weigh her down. A child's coat, and a child's hood.

'Goodbye, Patty,' he mumbled awkwardly, 'goodbye now, and thank you.'

'Goodbye, Pat Larry Dineen.' She reached up her hand and shook his. 'I'll see you again, Pat, I'll see you again. Soon.'

She waited until his van had vanished round the next turn, his big elbow reaching out the window. She waited until the sound of the engine had faded into the afternoon. There was silence, just a faint breeze around the corner of the church. She hadn't eaten for such a long time but she was not hungry. Somewhere in the fields a dog was barking. And once she heard the high, proud crowing of a cock. There was nobody on the roads, no sign of life from the scattered houses.

Inside the church she felt too weak to kneel. It was empty, but alive with echoes and dim, warm memories, and a fragrance, hovering, from years and years of incense and prayers and hope.

She sat in a quiet corner at the back, watching the small flickerings of the red lamp before the altar. She could not pray. She was too tired. Small flecks of light blue and turquoise shifted like moths with the living dance of clouds outside. She watched them play and fly over the walls inside the windows, she heard them sing.

A small bird flew in through the open door of the church. It flew rapidly through the vast empty universe of the building, disoriented, hurt, afraid. It came to rest at times and she watched it, pityingly. It landed near her once, its tiny, frightened eye momentarily focused on her. A thrush, she thought, the heart in the speckled breast thumping wildly. It had no cause to be frightened of her. She stretched out along the hard seat of the bench and fell quickly into a long, deep and untroubled sleep. Soon the bird, too, settled into a niche behind the confessional and grew still. The evening slipped by. It was night.

The church, when she woke, was a dark forest with one light shining, like a ray of sunshine, at the far end. She was stiff from the hard bench. When she tried to stand she realised that the pains had come upon her again. Every bone and muscle ached with the pain. She sat still for a long time, suffering it, and it eased, though slightly. She sat on, thinking. She could not present herself to Dodgie like this, a great rag of suffering that would be only a burden to him. And she could not go back, never back to that hospital where they took away her mind and put in its place a gurgling mess of insanity. She would hide, she would bury herself away from the world. Perhaps it had won then, at last, the wolf, perhaps it had won.

Someone had closed the back door and she could hear an uneasy, shifting, breathing sound from somewhere. She rose, painfully, and the bench hardly creaked under her lightness. She found a man asleep further up the forest, breathing loudly, shifting heavily. He looked lost and ill.

'You too,' she whispered at him. 'You too. Hiding from the beast. Yes, there are a lot of us. A lot of us.'

She walked unsteadily to the top of the church where the light was, and passed through the sacristy, out the door and into the churchyard. There was a full moon and the world was bathed in its uncertain light. The ground was wet after rain and a light breeze caught her with its coldness. She paused, to get her direction. Then she began to walk as quickly as she could, as if she had gained new strength and determination. At times she hesitated, as if she were missing something, something she should be carrying. The road passed through wild, empty moorland. In the distance she could see a strange glow behind the hills. Almost a beacon, she thought, calling her on. She could see fence and hillock and turf mound clearly under the moonlight.

'Buttercups, and dandelions, and daisies,' she said softly, 'daisies and dandelions and buttercups. Seagulls, too, and magpies. Magpies and bananas ...'

She stepped off the road and followed a turf path to the edge of a cut bog. She picked a few of the bog cotton flowers, gazing round her abstractedly. She put the flowers in the pocket of her red plastic coat and came back onto the road. She hurried on. The road was a grey ribbon ahead of her. She could see the lower reaches of the mountain. They were scarlet and red and orange, they shifted and wavered, like a mirage. She hurried on.

All afternoon they had moved across the mountain, slowly, determined. They had begun at the furthest end, where the mountain lifts quickly to its greatest height, leaving cliffs that stand up powerfully over the sea. They moved, spread out in a long line. They were armed with sticks, like clubs, with slash-hooks that were sharp and deadly, like machetes. They had pitchforks, like the tridents of the gladiators. They had knives. They had guns, too. They were cowboys and Indians, they were Tatars and Cossacks. The Captain was with them, silent, moving across the ground with a grim determination. He had his Mauser K98 rifle. He had loaded it, with one bullet, a German soldier's gift, a silver bullet.

They were dressed for the rough terrain and for the weather. Windcheaters. Belted overcoats. Raincoats. Caps. Hats. Waders. Studded boots. There were thirty, perhaps forty men. As they moved in their long chain, each man was close enough to be a support to another on either side of him. They moved in silence, except for an occasional call, an occasional word of encouragement. They beat the ground here and there as they passed. No living creature lifted before their march. They did not see bird, or sheep or goat along the mountain acres. Once, as dusk made every mound and hump into a wild beast poised to spring, one of the men lifted his rifle quickly and shot. The bullet went deep into a turf bank. The shot echoed over the mountainside and the calls of the man were frantic for a time. Then they all settled back into silence.

'Aiming at shadows, as usual,' the Captain commented.

Behind their long slow line came another line, ten men who carried on their backs great spraying cans filled with petrol. At intervals they covered the heathers and lings and grasses with a fine spray. And they, too, moved on.

All afternoon they moved across the mountain. They paused, in the early evening, to eat their sandwiches, to sip from their flasks of tea. Some of them took swift, burning gulps of whiskey. Fortifying their minds against whatever beast. Soon, as the first darkness came towards them, they were descending the easy slopes on the other side of the mountain. By late evening they stopped again to finish their food, to drain their flasks dry. They were tired now and irritable. They had found nothing.

About a mile behind them the fires followed. They began slowly, catching with a sudden whoosh of flames and settling to a small but steady vermilion glow that stretched the width of the mountainside. There was a growling, crackling sound as the dry heathers caught and burned. There were clouds of smoke drifting into the sky. It was as if the mountain muttered and cursed to itself.

The Captain turned and topped again a ridge he felt that had not been thoroughly explored. It was dark but the moon had risen and a mercury gleam touched the tussocks and the high crags of the mountain. Higher up he could see the rough edges of the northern slope, cliffs and crags that had been viciously torn in some great landfall years before. And then, the Captain would swear for ever after that he was certain, absolutely certain, a big shifting shape had loomed into the night between him and the mountain's slopes. A shape, a shadow, huge and menacing. And the stench of death and rottenness had assaulted his nostrils as a low wailing sound seemed to hang on the air all about him. He swore, too, that the shape had begun to move towards him, and for a long time the Captain was a stone, stiff and hopeless and alone. Suddenly the moon had fallen away behind a cloud and the darkness fell like a slap against the Captain's face and he had lifted the rifle and had aimed, his hands strangely steady, and he had fired. The report echoed wildly amongst the rocks and higher slopes and for a long moment there was nothing, emptiness only, hollowness, and cold.

The Captain could see the glow beyond from the fires along the mountain. He thought he saw a shape, human or animal he could not tell. He heard a call, he thought, a low, long-held call of pain, and then it disappeared, over the side of the cliff or into the great welcoming arms of the fire. The Captain could not tell. He could not tell. When they pressed him, later, he was not sure, how could he be sure, how could any of them ever know, ever again?

The whole flank of the mountain was in flames, the fire would burn for hours, gratefully, as if something was filling its terrible greed for destruction. The Captain stumbled quickly back towards the men. No, they had heard nothing, they had seen nothing, they had not heard him shoot, they had not heard a scream. He was imagining things, that's all. Shooting at shadows. He showed them the gun, the breach, the emptiness, one of them even touched the warm barrel. But tomorrow, after Mass, they would come again in a long line, crossing the mountainside more quickly, searching for exposed hollows they might have missed, searching for caverns or caves, for remains, they hoped, of what they thought was their prey.

She began the ascent of the lower slopes. The dancing reds and oranges and scarlets were far enough away to allow her climb. She strode out fearlessly over the rough ground. The pain was inside her, patient now, waiting, like the phoenix, to be reborn. Now and then a faint scent of burning touched her nostrils. She would have to hurry. She knew a strength now she had not known for some time. The moon showed rocks and waterlogged areas of the climb. She could hear her own footsteps over the hard ground. The light gleamed off the stones of a collapsed hut and she paused for a moment to rest. There were fallen stones dying back into the earth. There were small colonies of nettles growing among them. As she stood there, gazing back over the distance she had already come, her small body straight, the wellingtons too large for her feet, she knew a rich calmness, like the great calm of the spaces between the stars. She was determined. She knew her direction. She felt happy. She smiled on the silver landscape of her island.

Then she continued the climb. She reached a ridge of the mountain and down to her right she could make out the ocean, beautiful, still, under the moonlight. There was a strong scent now from the burning heathers but soon, she knew, soon she would cross another ridge and pass out of the reach of the breeze. There was a small valley, wet and covered in rushes and heathers. She crossed it lightly, like a butterfly, her red plastic coat gleaming like wings. 'All the better to see you with...' Then she was climbing again, a stiff climb, beginning to reach towards the higher slopes. She found this difficult, her breathing was harder, small aches beginning again in her limbs, a slight throbbing of pain in her temples. She topped another ridge high above the valley. Down to her right she could make out the lake, a pool of mercury in the embrace of the mountain. Here the breeze had ceased. She could no longer smell the fires. She paused, breathing deeply.

They came down, despondent, from the mountain. In almost total silence they gathered at the cars, taking off their heavy clothes, laying aside their weapons. They had found nothing. Nothing. It was dark now although a beautiful moon hung high above them. A wind was beginning to rise. There were premonitory drops of rain.

The Captain put his gun into the boot of his car. He was relieved to put it away again, out of his hands. Its weight had grown almost unbearable as the long afternoon had dragged into evening. As if he were hauling the weight of all the wars of the sorry world, there, in that old German gun he had cleaned and readied for the day.

He looked back up the mountain slopes. Soon, he knew, like a line of infantry, the fire would top the mountain and begin its inexorable descent down this side. A whole mountain on fire, he thought, it would be a night they would talk about for years to come. And he had convinced himself, too, that he had fought a shadow, that his silver bullet had fallen harmlessly into the soft flesh of the mountainside. For a moment he remembered Patty; he would see her soon, he would take joy in telling her of this expedition, he would watch her big eyes open wide as he told of the mountain on fire, of the glow, of the crackle, as of a million marching ants across a wooden floor. He would tell her of his bravery as he had faced alone into single combat with a shadow. She would laugh, and his heart would fill up with love and sorrow and with hope.

Poor old Dodgie. Poor Dodgie. As she began to move again she got a strong new scent on the air, a gentle fragrance, a musk, insinuating, all-pervasive. She began, very slowly, to climb further up the slope. As she climbed the fragrance seemed to grow stronger, more familiar, but she could not name it. A great coil of smoke passed above her, like a cloud against the moon, and she paused, disoriented. A sharp pain caught her right hand and she looked down at it; it had stiffened out again, the joints taut and brittle, the hand faint and white and trembling in the darkness. It had remained patient long enough, she knew. Now it was coming to take her. She thought she heard a low cry very far away. A cry of intense pain. It was her own cry, she believed, echoing far within herself. She hurried on, upwards, upwards.

At last she reached the final ridge. She could hear the loud crackling now of fires; she could even sense the heat from burning ferns and heathers. There was a harsh burning pain in her hand; her limbs felt, too, as if they were beginning to burn. Then she glimpsed them, a row of terrifying, strange-looking, silent figures stretched out in a row in the distance, moving slowly, slowly, slowly. Moving towards her. Frightening her. She found the ferns and grasses that hid an opening. She went on her hands and knees and pressed forward. At once she was in deep darkness. The earth underneath her was fine and firm. The cave roof was low, the entrance small but there was ample space for her body.

There was a total earth silence about her now. It was dark beyond belief. But the earth was dry and soon she found she could stand up, her hair just touching the roof of the cave. A sense of that earlier fragrance lingered about her. She could hear only her own small breathing.

The cave seemed to take a sharp turn to her right. She moved cautiously, her hands extended, touching the earth on either side. She reached an end wall. She turned and sat on the earth, her back against the wall. She was not cold. The pains in her limbs were intense but she would not cry out. The pain within her head was growing, too, she felt as if all the pain she had ever known would pound within her head for a time, urgent to get out. But in spite of all of that she was at peace, lucid and calm and at peace. She smiled into the darkness. She closed her eyes and sank into her own richer darkness. She drew her knees up against her stomach, put her arms about her knees and bent her head down to rest. She was an embryo of pain. She was at peace. She waited.